# The Calabash of Coral Island and Other Early Stories

Other book collections by Arthur Porges:

*Three Porges Parodies and a Pastiche* (1988)
*The Mirror and Other Strange Reflections* (2002)
*Eight Problems in Space: The Ensign De Ruyter Stories* (2008)
*The Adventures of Stately Homes and Sherman Horn* (2008)

Forthcoming titles by Arthur Porges:

*The Miracle of the Bread and Other Stories*
*The Devil and Simon Flagg and Other Fantastic Tales*
*The Ruum and Other Science Fiction Stories*
*The Collected Essays of Arthur Porges*

# The Calabash of Coral Island and Other Early Stories

## Arthur Porges

### Edited by Richard Simms

Richard Simms Publications

This paperback first edition published in 2008

Richard Simms Publications, Surrey, England

ISBN: 978-0-9556942-0-2

*With special thanks to Sue Wakefield, Cele Porges and Joel Hoffman.*

For more information please visit The Arthur Porges Fan Site:

http://arthurporges.atwebpages.com

# Contents

# Introduction

In the summer of 2006, some weeks after my dear friend and literary hero Arthur Porges left the world, I was honored to discover from his sister-in-law, Cele Porges, that Arthur had bequeathed to me a certain amount of his papers. Overwhelmed and excited by this privilege, I silently thanked Arthur and, upon receiving the papers, went about the task of reading and sorting through them. The material did not look like it was in any kind of order, but I refused to be daunted by what appeared to be a somewhat large amount of miscellaneous writings!

Perhaps the most intriguing item of all consisted of a thick sheaf of yellowing, typewritten manuscripts held together by rusty metal rods. Upon opening the file—carefully—it soon became clear that what I had inherited was a treasure trove of unpublished, hitherto-undiscovered manuscripts. It was also quickly apparent that most of these papers dated from long before Arthur Porges was ever published. The literary treasures I beheld consisted of plays, scripts, humorous sketches, comedies, book reviews, essays, poems ... and, to my particular delight, several of Arthur's early experiments in short fiction.

Such were the contents of this old file of papers; material dating way back to the 1930s and 1940s. The short stories in this collection are wholly derived from this source material, comprising previously unpublished tales written, as noted above, years before Porges sold his first short story.

In the early thirties Arthur Porges was a teenager living in Chicago with his father and three brothers. After finishing High School, he attended The Illinois Institute of Technology, from which he gained a degree in Mathematics. Always a lover of science, his extensive reading of fact and fiction inspired him to take up writing. Several of the stories in this collection date specifically from a period in the mid-1930s when the young Mr. Porges was taking a college writing course. These manuscripts, written purposefully for various themes set for the class as part of the course, are invariably inscribed with marginal notes and marked with overall grades by an unnamed teacher—who clearly thought highly of Arthur's contributions. I will note here that the teacher recognized his pupil's talent; Arthur's stories, essays and humorous plays scored straight A's throughout!

Unfortunately, the English professor in question, who gave Porges so much encouragement and valued advice, will probably forever remain anonymous. Throughout our correspondence, Arthur never mentioned him. In fact, he did not talk very much about his college days at all. Of course, I had asked him about his early influences, and was aware that before 1950 he had, for years, been trying without success to sell his short stories to various periodicals. But I was simply not cognizant, until after he passed away, that any such early unpublished manuscripts actually existed. Therefore I was absolutely thrilled to unearth such a wealth of interesting material.

Around half the stories presented here are drawn from manuscripts written as part of the aforementioned college course. The other stories in this volume are nearly all taken from the post-war period of the late 1940s, when Arthur was living at a North Albany Avenue address in his hometown of Chicago, Illinois. This was the period subsequent to his time in the U.S. Army where he served in an artillery division as an instructor and came out a First Lieutenant. This was also the time prior to his making a permanent move to California, where he taught Mathematics at various colleges and also embarked on his published writing career, starting in 1950.

Both the post-war stories and the earlier yarns penned during his college days, are presented here for the very first time. They can be seen as a chronicle of a young author developing his style and finding his own unique literary voice. Those dating from the late 1940s, where Arthur's increasing maturity as a writer is evident, show a more polished style—certainly the mss themselves are presented in a more professional, editor-friendly manner! At this point he was getting close to his first sale and the quality, in terms of both content and presentation, is high. But there are stories from each of these periods that stand up well against his later, generally more accomplished works. What we have here is a selection of highly individualistic stories by an author who took his ideas from all kinds of sources. From the outset, as one will see, Porges exhibited a true gift for spinning imaginative and entertaining yarns. These stories show us that he was a born storyteller.

I have resisted the temptation to indulge in an exhaustive and possibly tiresome discussion, analysis and blow-by-blow account of each of the twenty-one stories gathered in this volume. Rather, I will concentrate—for the most part—in this introduction on those stories where I trust I can provide some background and—I hope—offer a few insights. It is also important, I feel, to attempt to put these tales into some kind of context, both in terms of Arthur's life, and his later career as a writer. I would advise those impatient with facts and background detail to skip my introductory notes—if they haven't already—and get on with reading the stories!

The first story in this book is also the earliest of Arthur's manuscripts to survive to the present day. The original manuscript for "The Crabs of Coral Island," written when Porges was eighteen years old, is dated May 21, 1934. The exotic setting for this story is a small, isolated island in the South Pacific. This story, like its sequel "The Calabash of Coral Island," takes the form of a monologue, narrated by an acquaintance of "Dutch" Vandermeer, a European trader and adventurer who one pictures as a tall, bronzed, athletic man who has seen it all. The two stories that make up this series are second-hand accounts of peculiar happenings on the island witnessed by

Vandermeer. These tales are never less than interesting and show Arthur's love of the strange and unusual in fiction.

From the Pacific, we move to Europe and the strange, offbeat comedy of "Mind or Matter." Another tale from the 1930s, it follows the unfortunate demise of one Professor Addlewitz, Doctor of all Doctors of Philosophy, of the University of Nuremburg. This story is quite intentionally ludicrous and is an early example of Porges' talent for spinning humorous yarns.

"Was Peters' Watch Right?" is an engaging story of a group of miners trapped by a cave-in. An exercise in suspense, this intriguing tale boasts some excellent dialogue and a clever gimmick at the end, where the reader is asked to decide the answer to the question of the title.

The fable-like social satire "The Glass House Cure," and the rather touching romance story "The Coward," the latter about a man who finally overcomes his timidity, are likewise interesting, but at heart, intensely serious; it should also be noted that they are quite unlike anything else in the Porges canon. It is perhaps this latter quality that is part of their fascination. The same could be said for "The Peasant Madonna," about an artist struggling to finish his last painting, and "Seaside Flirtation," a delicate tale of a young man's encounter with a mermaid on a secluded beach. The seasonal "Pierre Renard's Christmas," which is both evocative and heartwarming, is particularly well written and I am especially pleased to be able to present it here.

Interestingly, all of the above tales have, to a greater or lesser degree, a supernatural element. The quality of strangeness that pervades these stories was no doubt inspired by Porges' love of fantastic fiction. It was, after all, around this time that he discovered *Weird Tales* magazine, having already devoured the imaginative output of such authors as H. Rider Haggard and Rudyard Kipling.

One of the longest stories in this collection, an outrageous spoof set among the ancient Greek gods entitled "The True Story of Hercules," is a fantasy of an altogether different nature. It could be argued that this is more of a humorous sketch than a story. It is packed with imaginative set pieces and deliciously cutting verbal exchanges between the assorted deities of antiquity, who, in Porges' version of the old legend, consistent with tradition, do not get on too well with one another. Thus, we have various divinities getting the hump and endlessly bickering, to great comedic effect. Zeus is to be seen hurling thunderbolts in anger as he waits for his dinner, while the youngest of the Three Graces is upset at all the slang words being thrown about! As for poor Hercules himself, he is portrayed as a stolid, resourceful, yet sensitive chap who is continually put upon by his fellow celestials and is thoroughly disenchanted with his lot in life.

Porges' idiosyncratic retelling of the Greek myth was one of those tales he wrote while at college. The unnamed teacher, ever appreciative, called it "delightful nonsense." I heartily agree. The original manuscript of this story also bears the following marginal comment: "I shall be sorry to lose these contributions of yours." So, "The True Story of Hercules," possibly the most surprising and atypical of all these stories, was one of the last of the writing course era.

"The Tooth," is a supernatural horror story set, on this occasion, in modern Greece. As this disquieting little tale progresses, however, it becomes evident that an ancient legend is about to impinge upon the present day, with terrible consequences for the hapless archaeologist who uncovers an object that he should have left well alone.

The vignette "Return to Me," is one of those stories from the late 1940s, an elegant and affecting piece that is incomparable to any of Porges' other tales. Quite frankly, it comes straight out of left field. A wartime love story about a soldier writing home to his beloved, the one-page manuscript for this poignant tale not only lacked a date, or an address, but was even missing a title! Now, I read somewhere that finding a suitable title for a story can be a more challenging task to writers than the job of composing the story itself. It is possible that Arthur just didn't bother with a title; I suspect he didn't try to sell this one; a pity, as newspapers and magazines were snapping up little gems like this in the 1940s. That aside, in trying to think up a suitable title, I found myself stumped. How do you encapsulate a story like this in a few words—words that are to shine at the top of the story like a beacon light? Nothing I came up with seemed to fit. Thankfully, my partner Sue came to the rescue, suggesting what I trust you'll agree is an appropriate, evocative title. I like to think Arthur would have approved of "Return to Me." The period piece that now bears this name is one of my personal favorites in this book.

The much longer "The Surgical Cracksman and the Crime School," an adventure thriller set in the criminal underworld, is rather unnerving. It follows the ordeal of Doctor Godfrey van Nuys, a surgeon who in his spare time is also an expert safecracker. Forced against his will to undergo several initiation tests before joining the "Crime School" of the title, van Nuys' ingenuity is ruthlessly tested until the suspense builds up to an exciting climax. There is more than a hint of romance in this tale, but a particularly disturbing execution scene offsets this element, engendering a sense of unease. The interest, drama, and excitement are effectively sustained, but I think this is one of those stories that will divide opinion among readers. The question, in my view, is whether Porges succeeds in making what happens convincing; the reader may make up his own mind.

The story that follows is more typical of Porges. The unsettling "A Dictator Dies," a dark, uncompromising revenge story with a murderous twist at the end—the method used is based on a little known fact of science—is briskly told and competently handled.

"When the Sleeper Wakes" is a kind of condensed western story. The action takes place in a saloon bar, where frayed tempers lead to a violent confrontation. I know of no other westerns by Porges, but this one is handled brilliantly. The dialogue is sharp as a razor's edge and the hardboiled tone is complemented perfectly by some delightful black humor: "... you folks don't seem to realize the value of sleep!"

There is certainly no chance of dozing off to the tightly written and utterly captivating "A Quick Death," a slow motion, intensely detailed depiction of the journey of a bullet into a suicide's brain. The death described in this chilling and masterful story is not so quick when one's time-sense is thrown out of kilter, as it is here, in one of the very best stories in this volume.

The following four stories gathered here are Arthur's earliest forays into the field of science fiction. The grim, end of the world story "No Survivors" is another yarn dating from the writing course

Porges attended in the mid-1930s. I see from the tutor's notes scribbled on the last page that this tale was shown to other students of English 16. The teacher remarks that many of them were unconvinced by the ending, although otherwise it was generally considered a good, "dramatically told" story.

"The Terror of the Mindanao Depths" is, in this writer's opinion, an altogether more accomplished tale—if a trifle over-ambitious in theme. This one was written much later; it dates from the late 1940s, hence the quantum leap in quality. It's another one of those orphaned stories that lacked a title, so the unashamedly barnstorming "The Terror of the Mindanao Depths" can be blamed on me! It is certainly the longest story in this book and, indeed one of the longest that Porges ever wrote. The story is narrated by one of the central characters, Glenn Lambert, an expert on marine life. As Lambert, Gunnarson and McAllister descend into the ocean depths, one is conscious that this story was surely inspired by the early science fiction adventures of H. G. Wells, Arthur Conan Doyle and Jules Verne. It certainly has something of the spirit of such novels as *20,000 Leagues Under the Sea*, *The Time Machine*, *The Lost World* and *Journey to the Center of the Earth* about it. McAllister's "Thought-Compass," able to detect a malevolent mental presence in the Mindanao Deep, is a clever idea. The story is packed with fascinating scientific and technical detail. Porges' invention and skill as a writer of imaginative fiction is on display here in this absorbing tale. The undersea scenes, with the imagined creatures of the hitherto-uncharted ocean depths described in vivid detail, are expertly handled. This story packs a real punch, but it is fair to say that within a few years Porges had progressed from writing rip-roaring, old-fashioned adventures such as these. "The Terror of the Mindanao Depths" stands as a kind of homage by Porges to the early masters of science fiction, whose writings so fired his imagination as a young man.

The plot and characters of "Denizens of the Drop" are of secondary importance. A scientist and his son are miniaturized in a laboratory and placed among the tiny organisms that inhabit a drop of water under a microscope. This charming, fast-paced story from the 1930s reads as an authoritative guide to microscopic life. With typical attention to detail, Porges gives us authentic descriptions of such microscopic organisms as the Paramecium, the Euglena, the Didinium and the more commonly known Amoebae.

"Monsters of the Grasslands" also features a human who has been miniaturized. This is hardly a startlingly original concept, but that fact barely matters. The focus of this story is, similarly, Porges' fascinating, intricate, and realistic descriptions of nature. Porges succeeds in imbuing a sense of wonder in this story, where this time, a man is shrunk to the size of an ant and attempts to survive among the insect life. It is worth noting that the authentic detail on display here was derived from certain essays contained in the complete English edition of Jean-Henri Fabre's *Souvenirs Entomologiques*.

The exact same source material provided the authenticity for the final story in this collection, "The Soulless Ones: Vespa," which Arthur aptly described as "fictionalized fact." This remarkable piece was written during the Second World War, when First Lieutenant Porges was stationed in Vancouver, Washington. There are no miniaturized humans this time, just a thrilling, true-to-life, painstakingly researched story of a hunting wasp. The encounter with a praying mantis, and the quite horrible aftermath, is described to chilling effect. Arthur Porges' knowledge—in this case gleaned from Fabre's famous work—of natural history and the sometimes harsh, uncomfortable truths of nature, is displayed here to full, superb effect.

The title of this story suggests that it may have been part of a series, but alas, it would seem that no others were written. I suspect that Porges abandoned the idea of writing a whole series of "Soulless Ones" stories, which is a pity. He did, however, write several more nature stories, which happily *were* published. "Eight Legged Monster" (*Boys' Life*, August 1952) and "By a Fluke" (*The Magazine of Fantasy and Science Fiction*, October 1955) are somewhat akin in nature to "The Soulless Ones: Vespa" and I heartily recommend them—they are well worth searching out. Another later animal story, "The Black Tyrant" (*Boys' Life*, September 1955), about a raven, is also quite excellent. One wishes he had written more in this vein.

But with "The Soulless Ones: Vespa," an accomplished, satisfying tale which amply exhibits several of Porges' hallmark qualities as a writer of short fiction, we end this collection on a high. This story and indeed several others assembled here do more than merely hint at the greatness that was to come; they are outstanding and accomplished works in themselves.

The book you are holding in your hands is probably best viewed as a chronicle of an author's early exercises in short story writing. The stories selected for this volume represent the beginnings of a talent that was to emerge into the published world several years later. The extraordinary range of genres and themes on display here should ensure there is something for everyone to enjoy. I believe each story has its own special charm, and the reader will no doubt have his own favorites among the variety of tales included in this collection.

I hope you enjoy these stories. So find a comfortable chair, relax, and lose yourself in outlandish settings and unusual situations, as seen through the eyes of the young Arthur Porges. Experience unique places you would, perhaps, otherwise never have visited. In stories that never saw the light of day. At least until now. Thank you, Arthur.

*Richard Simms*
*Surrey, England*
*March, 2008*

# The Crabs of Coral Island

It was on the occasion of my last visit to "Dutch" Vandermeer's trading post on Coral Island, a tiny bit of land near the Yasawa Group off the Fiji Islands, that I heard this story. Dutch has been making a living off the trusting natives for thirty-two lonesome years, having first set foot upon the island in 1901. It may seem odd that a man could make any sort of a decent living on a speck like Coral Island, but the fact is, that what with coconut trees supplying copra, and natives supplying pearls—for a consideration—Dutch made what could be termed a comfortable living. Still, it ain't no pleasant life, living on a tiny island with only natives and coconut crabs for companions. There are great numbers of these crabs, the reason for which you shall see.

I made Dutch's acquaintance when a ship on which I was the second, chanced to stop there for repairs. I had hardly set foot on shore before a slip of a native girl told me that a white man was dying of the fever. Of course, I think it's only a beachcomber, but after all … well, you know how it is. So I went over to the little hut the girl pointed out, and there I found Dutch. He was down pretty bad with malaria, and he didn't have no more quinine—a deadly combination. Luckily we had some on board, and to make it short, I nursed him back to health, and since then, he and I have been pretty thick. Every time my ship—I'm her skipper now—anchors at Coral Island, as she does every few months, I drop in and have a catch up with Dutch. And, believe you me, he knows of plenty yarns of the type my French third mate would call "outré." Anyway, here's the story.

It seems that Dutch and a few of his native help were sorta strolling along the beach, looking for likely pearling grounds, when one of the men taps Dutch on the shoulder. When he looks where the fellow's pointing, he can just make out a small ship's boat drifting their way. Right away he has a native swim out and bring it in. In the bottom of it is a white man, more than half dead by the looks of him. Dutch gets some fresh water quick, and dipping a clean rag into it, puts a few drops down the guy's mouth by squeezing, nice and gently. Pretty soon the fellow groans feebly and asks where he is. Dutch tells him, and the guy swears, then conks out again.

The natives carry the unconscious man to Dutch's hut and give him food and water, a little at a time so as not to hurt him. It turns out that his name is John Scrivens, able seaman, and that he's been drifting for five days since his ship, *The Pride of Liverpool*, foundered during a typhoon. He says that most of the other fellows in the boat with him were washed out, and that the rest went nutty and jumped out. Dutch believed it then, but since, he and I think differently.

Well, at the end of a couple of days, this guy's trotting around the place like he'd never been adrift a day, but when Dutch hints gently that he do something to earn his keep, he plays dumb. But that ain't the only thing about him what Dutch don't like.

On Coral Island, just like on a lotta other islands in the Pacific, are these big crabs they call coconut crabs. They're great big ones, sometimes a foot across, and as a rule they eat only coconuts. They climb a tree, usually in the morning, nip off a ripe nut at the stem, climb back down, and after crunching off the end with their pinchers, drink the milk, and maybe eat some of the meat. They pack a lotta power in those pinchers, and if a native finds one of them in the top of a tree, the native goes down. The crabs don't do Dutch's coconut trade no good, but outside of killing a few now and then to keep their numbers down, Dutch let them alone.

But this guy Scrivens seems to hate the animals, and after he's been on Coral Island a couple of weeks, you could see their crushed shells all over the place. This burns Dutch up, because he's the kind of guy who won't kill unless he has to, and furthermore, Scrivens is not over kind to the natives, either. But Mr. Scrivens is a fellow European, and Dutch, out of a misguided sense of loyalty, treats him square.

One day a diver brings Dutch a monster pearl, the kind he's been dreaming about for years. A new pearling spot has been found where the giant pearl oysters ain't never been touched—and how the beauties keep coming in! Meanwhile, Scrivens has been sending long letters by the mail boat what comes once a month, and has been receiving answers just as long, postmarked "Liverpool."

Then one day the break comes. A native going by with a load of nuts, stumbles over Scrivens' outstretched feet and drops the heavy bag on him. Scrivens gets up, his little eyes blazing, and hits the fellow a terrific crack in the mouth. The native drops like a log and gets a boot in the ribs.

Dutch, who has seen the whole thing, tears out madder than a hornet, but Scrivens reads murder in his eyes and digs into his pocket, whipping out a heavy automatic.

"Stand where you are, Dutch!" he snaps. "I'm taking no chances."

Dutch remains motionless, his face void of expression. Only his eyes narrow and become watchful. "You sneaking rat," he says thickly.

Scrivens grins. "Never mind the pet names, Dutch," he says. "It's the pearls I want."

"You'll never get 'em," grits Dutch.

The smile fades from Scrivens' face. Suddenly he raises the gun and fires pointblank. Dutch's arm drops to his side, broken, and his brown face whitens from the pain. But still he stands quiet.

"I'm waiting," grates Scrivens.

"You can't get off the island, anyway," snaps Dutch angrily, swaying a little on his feet.

"Think not?" Scrivens sneers. "My pals will be waiting for me in the sweetest little ship you ever seen. I'll borrow your launch to get aboard her. Now get them pearls!"

Dutch doesn't move, his jaw set. Scrivens grins a crooked grin and waves his gun at a native. "Tie him up!" he orders. Trembling, the native ties Dutch to the rough bole of a big coconut palm.

"If you know what's good for you, you'll talk," says Scrivens, once Dutch is securely bound. He comes close to him and examines the bonds; he ain't taking no chances. "I know a few Chinese tricks," he says, pulling a wicked little knife from his pocket, "what'll make you talk, and talk fast!"

Then it happens. From the thick foliage above, a round object streaks down and hits Scrivens' head with a sickening "thuck!" He stands straight for a moment and then topples without a sound. Beside him is a large, ripe coconut. For a few seconds there is no sound. Then they hear a scratching, rasping noise, and slowly and clumsily a big coconut crab sidles down the trunk of the palm. At the bottom it calmly drops off, stands for a minute twitching its antennae, then goes over to the coconut. After favoring Scrivens with a suspicious glance, the crab proceeds to crack off the end of the nut and begin its meal. The native turns Dutch loose immediately. Scrivens is dead as a duck—a heavy coconut dropping from an eighty-five foot tree is enough to finish off an elephant.

And that's why the coconut crabs are so plentiful on Coral Island. Dutch weighs two hundred and ten pounds in his stockinged feet, and nobody dares touch 'em!

# The Calabash of Coral Island

My friend, "Dutch" Vandermeer, who has a trading post on Coral Island, a little speck of land near the Yasawa Group in the Pacific Ocean, has seen and heard a good many strange things during his thirty-odd years of isolation. Whenever I drop down to see him, which I does occasionally, he has some kind of yarn to spin.

A good many of these stories sound a little wild even to me, but never having tripped Dutch up, and knowing him like I do, I believe every word he says.

This is a tale Dutch told me one stifling night when the great yellow moon was hanging down low and weary like. Maybe that's why it impressed me so.

Every month the mail boat stops at Coral Island to drop mail and newspapers and such. Once in a blue moon there's a passenger. Maybe a psalm-singer stops off to convert Dutch's natives, or maybe a scout for some pearling company hangs around for a few days.

One day the boat wheezes into port and lets off a short dreamy looking guy who's porting a lot of weighty baggage. His name turns out to be Graham T. Williams, and he's a professor of Philology at some big college in the States.

Well, first off, Dutch drags out his Webster and looks up the word "Philology." You see, he don't run into them kinda words very often, not having had my education. Anyway, he found out that it means the study of languages. This Williams ain't very secretive, and Dutch soon worms out the fact that he's looking for some of the stuff mentioned in the Island legends.

It seems that the professor is particularly interested in a certain calabash, or container, reputed to have been buried by a great medicine man of the island centuries before. When Dutch questions him, he acts embarrassed, and finally admits that the calabash is supposed to contain some of the Elixir of Life. Can you tie that! Naturally, he expects Dutch to give him the laugh, but Dutch has been in them parts long enough to consider anything possible. Not only that, but he's so interested that he introduces Williams to the native big shots, and as he's always treated them square, they're glad to take to a friend of his.

In fact they like him so well, that they stuff him with food of unknown origin and quality. Dutch is also plumb astounded when he hears this professor talk to them in their own language like he'd talked it all his life. In a couple of weeks they're telling him things they wouldn't tell their own grandmothers! And Dutch is not a little jealous.

From a real ancient native, who knows all there is to be known about the legends, Williams finally finds out where the calabash is said to be buried.

The natives advise him strongly to leave it lay, but of course he won't listen. Who would? Since he can't get them to take him to the spot for love or money, he elects Dutch to be his guide, and strangely enough Dutch don't raise no objections.

You see, there's something about this Elixir of Life business that has fired human imagination for hundreds of years. You remember that old Spanish bird Ponce de Leon, and how anxious he was to find it? So you can't blame Dutch for being a little excited.

Well, they starts out, packing all the necessary supplies, including a pick and shovel. Professor Williams also has a sketchy map made by the old native. The location is about a two-day journey from Dutch's place, but they makes it in half a day less. Williams is in a pretty bad way when they finally arrive. He's not used to that sort of country, and even tough old Dutch ain't feeling too perky.

Once there, Williams putters nervously about, interpreting the weird signs on the map, and finally points a shaking finger at the spot where they're to dig. Together they make the rich earth fly, and the hole gets deeper and deeper. Suddenly Dutch's pick hits something that sounds hollow, and they almost kill one another clawing it out.

The professor gets it first though. It's a medium-sized rotten box. Eagerly, Williams rips apart the termite-ridden wood. Inside is a large calabash, covered with some rubbery composition.

Williams almost went out of his head with excitement. With trembling hands he claws the rubbery stuff off one end. He can hear the liquid gurgling as he works, and his eyes are plenty wild. Suddenly the cover comes free in his hand, and at the same time, Dutch sees with horror a great spider crawl out of the centuries-old container. Immediately it buries its black fangs in Williams' hand. With a cry of pain, the professor dropped the calabash. The action was not intended; Williams would far rather have had his hand eaten off than drop it, but reflex action did the trick, and the loamy soil sucked up the Elixir in a flash.

Now Williams did go batty, and it takes Dutch four terrible days to get him back to the post, where he eventually recovered. But he was a broken man.

In proof of this yarn, which sounds so wild, Dutch often shows me a little red flower, a weed-pest of the island that received the majority of the spilled liquid. According to Dutch's Botany Dictionary, it is an annual plant—that is, it lives but one year. But that little red flower still grows and flourishes in the same spot where Williams spilled the Elixir on it twenty-two years ago.

# Mind or Matter

It is with a heavy heart that I take my pen in hand to write of the sad sequence of events that led to the death of the greatest scientific genius the world has ever known. I refer, of course, to the late Professor Theobald Otto Gottfried von Addlewitz, Doctor of all Doctors of Philosophy, and my respected and revered teacher.

That his death should have occurred before the completion of his momentous mathematical work, which consisted in part of a translation into Esperanto of the General Theory of Relativity, makes all mathematicians feel the loss more keenly.

But my grief is tempered with pride, for the worthy doctor proved, by those same fatally terminating events, that mind is superior to matter.

I first met Professor Addlewitz at the University of Nuremburg, where he was giving semi-weekly lectures to a small group of advanced students, most of whom had long since passed the age of active resistance. The name of the text was "The Theory of the Theory of Theoretical Functional Functions," and to read the introduction alone would have given a fatal case of brain fever to any but an experienced mathematician.

However, after a short but fervent discussion with the dean, the president of the senior class—a most amiable centenarian—and a few conscienceless members of the freshman football squad, I finally admitted that the course might prove beneficial even to a student like myself, who intended to teach high school cooking.

And I had no cause to regret my wise decision, for after the first deft dissection of a wildly wiggling function I was Addlewitz's slave. What a fascinating personality he was! Whenever one of our weaker brethren fainted from a particularly sharp attack of functional nausea, the professor would quickly revive him with a moral little tale.

One of his favorites had to do with an explorer who was trapped in a cave. The unfortunate man had naught with him save three candles, and those he resolved to save for food lest a rescue party should be slow in arriving. Hours passed and the victim began to eat his candles; a bite or two of bland tallow every day. Gradually he felt his strength failing, and was about to kill himself in despair when the arrival of the rescuers proved him to have been imprisoned but three hours …

Doctor Addlewitz would enlarge upon this story, hug it, fondle it to his bosom, and invariably end by saying: "The body, that is nothing! The mind, that is the vital force!" Alas, how well he was to prove his point.

Having become in his leisure moments an authority on such varied subjects as cell division among ball-bearings, the probability of a hungry mosquito describing a parabola 212 times in succession—an ancient Hindu problem, that!—and prehistoric man, he was sent to investigate a recently discovered cave containing invaluable relics of the Cro-Magnon Man, his wife—who answered, in the absence of her husband, to the name Cro-Magnon Woman—and their children who were far, far, too numerous!

Leaving his guide in a fit of rage because the latter persisted in stating that one times zero must be one, because he could see where the one would slide through the zero if you pointed it right, Professor Addlewitz entered a series of ramifying passages. Eventually, he found himself trapped in a small chamber not unlike a rat trap, and a good deal damper. Unable to force his way out and with naught but a flashlight for sustenance, the worthy Doctor seated himself gently upon the dank floor to think a way out of his predicament.

"I must not make the mistake of the other explorer," he told himself calmly. "I've got to realize that a few minutes can seem like a very long time."

And so, this keen and intelligent thinker, this unparalleled logician, rested quietly upon the floor of what might turn out to be his tomb, and reviewed, with the aid of a geologist's hammer, the Morse Code, the International Morse Code, and the Universal Morse code.

The slow moments crawled wearily by and Addlewitz commenced to tap out all of Shakespeare's sonnets, the Iliad, the Chemical Dictionary (Thorpe's), and Professor Mille Tonnerre's "The Theory of the Theoretical Theory of all Theories," the latter a highly practical work that was easy to recall.

He even succeeded in teaching a few stray bats the Morse Code, a circumstance greatly puzzling to passing telegraphers, who heard emanating—apparently from solid rocks—such odd expressions as "Romeo, Romeo, wherefore art thou, Romeo?" and "An analytic function of an analytic function *is* an analytic function, if analytically and functionally defined for the analytic point in question."

After the passage of an indeterminate number of hours, there was a resounding crash, and through the film of rock that separated Theobald from light and air poked the battered front of a disheveled Buick. Seated in the car was a choleric, red-faced tourist.

"Who're you?" he demanded in astonishment.

"I," said the professor with not a little pride, "am Professor Theobald Otto Gottfried von Addlewitz, associated at present with the University of Nuremburg."

"Addlewitz! Nuremburg! I thought you looked familiar! Why, man, where've you been? They've been searching for you for three and a half years. The Mafia, the Black Hand and the Parent-Teacher's Association have each been accused of having a hand in your disappearance!"

Yes, incredulous reader, the worthy Herr Doctor had, by means solely of his powerful intellect, lived in a dank, dark cave for three and a half years without a bite to eat, and was as rotund and crusty as ever. Truly, mind is greater than matter!

But—alas for the loss to science—the above matter came out at the trial of the scoundrel tourist, who having in his butterfly college days suffered through Addlewitz's indigestible course in "The Art of Writing Iambic Hexadecameter Sonnets in Etruscan," put an end to the professor, who had fainted from the sudden onrush of fresh air, by tying a tourniquet tightly about his throat, and removing it only after the twenty minutes specified in his first aid manual.

I am sorry to have to report that the tourist was unanimously acquitted by a heartless jury of Nuremburg students, and was later awarded an honorary degree of Master of First Aid. Such is the reward of virtue!

# Was Peters' Watch Right?

Grunting heavily, the giant man drew back the weighty pick in preparation for another powerful slash at the ledge of crumbled anthracite. The great muscles rolled under his sweaty skin, and he bared his teeth with the effort of his stroke.

Abruptly he halted his swing and listened intently. His keen ears had caught an odd, distant sound—a faint and far away rumbling. Even as he gained his feet, the rumbling swelled to a roar, and the roar to a deafening thunder. To the men working in the narrow side passage leading off from Gallery 2, the noise could mean but one thing. Cave-in!

Flinging his pick to one side, the huge man ran at top speed down the dimly lighted passage, the coal roof of which was supported at intervals by great wooden beams. But as fast as he ran, he was too late. Even as he neared the end of the gallery, the caving roof began to exert its enormous pressure upon the outermost of the heavy wooden joists.

Stopping suddenly in his tracks, with his eyes rolling in their sockets, he saw the two supporting beams begin slowly to give way. Under the weight of countless tons of anthracite coal, the square pillars of seasoned maple creaked audibly. Then, ever so slowly they began to bend. There was a sharp snap as a great splinter shot from the right hand support. Instantly the whole structure gave way. Simultaneously with the resulting rumble, the lights went out, and the little passage was cut off from the rest of the mine—cut off by thousands of pounds of rock and coal.

For a moment there was no sound in the darkness save for the faint thudding made by tumbling bits of debris. Then a calm voice asked quietly if anybody had any matches. A few seconds later there was a scratching sound, and the pale glare of a safety match cast dancing shadows upon the black walls.

"Anybody injured?" inquired the possessor of the calm voice.

"I don't think so, sir," answered one of the men, after a peering glance about. "There's only six of us here, and we were all pretty far back. Good thing the rest of the supports held."

"Well, they did, and that's all that counts just now. Let's take stock. In the first place, being foreman, I'm still in command, so I'll take charge just as if nothing had happened."

"Mr. Peters," asked one of the men in a hoarse voice, "what do you think are the chances of a rescue party?"

"Quite good," Peters assured him in a voice far more confident than his private feelings warranted. "I don't think the cave-in occurred over a very large area, and they'll surely have a rescue party down here pretty soon."

"But, Boss, how about the air?" The giant, whose name was Briggs, put the question that all of them had feared to ask, even of themselves.

Peters cleared his throat. "Well," he said slowly, "I couldn't say exactly, but I'd venture to say that the air in here is good for six men, for about, well, two hours, providing of course that we take it easy."

With a warning flicker, the match went out. Cursing fluently as the glowing bit of wood scorched his finger, the man lit another.

Peters spoke sharply. "Put out that light!" he snapped. "One of those matches can use up more air than we can!"

"But ... stay in the dark, sir?" protested the wizened miner who had lit it.

"Afraid of the bogeyman?" snarled the foreman. "Don't be a pack of chumps! If you'd sooner choke than be in the dark, I don't give a tinker's damn, but I'd advise you to consider first!"

The men accepted the common sense of Peters' statement, and when the second match went out, no one lit a third.

The silence remained unbroken for some time. Then the big man began to moan softly.

"Who is that?" called Peters sharply. "What's the trouble?"

"My hand," came Briggs' muttered reply. "A big piece of rock smashed into it, and man, it sure does hurt."

"Why in hell didn't you say so?" stormed the foreman. "Do you want to get blood poisoning?" Even as he asked the question he realized its absurdity. Fat chance there'd be of the big guy dying of blood poisoning. He wouldn't live that long. No use voicing such thoughts, though.

"Light up another match," he ordered, tearing a piece from his once white shirt as he did so. By the feeble yellow light, he examined the fellow's injured member and silently bandaged it. "Now keep quiet, and go to sleep, if you can."

"Thanks, Boss," said the huge miner, with gratitude showing in his eyes through the pain.

"Okay," returned Peters, gruffly, as he walked back to his corner.

To remain silent was impossible, so the men began to converse in whispers. The lowering of the voices was entirely a psychological effect; there was no need for such caution.

Briggs was now singing softly to himself. The words of "Swing Low, Sweet Chariot" came dolefully from his lips, and one by one, the men added their voices to his, until the low roof of the black chamber began to resound with the rich notes.

Peters was in a quandary. Well he knew that the singing would serve only to use up more quickly their meager supply of air. On the other hand, if the men did not sing, their minds might be directed along more morbid lines.

The foreman had once seen a huge Norwegian, who had been brooding over a girl, run suddenly amok. He could picture the scene quite clearly. The men scattering with frightened cries, as the big yellow-haired worker ran silently after them, one brawny hand clutching his heavy sledgehammer. Luckily, due to his naturally well balanced mind, the man had returned abruptly to his senses and had been abjectly apologetic …

But here, conditions were different. Suppose that the giant man, maddened by the pain of his mangled hand, were to take his sharp steel pick and … Peters shuddered and dismissed the thought. Better let them sing; the poor devils might just as well go out that way.

Abruptly, some one exclaimed, and the foreman quickly lit a match. By its flickering orange flame he saw a burly Irishman striding toward him, holding of all things, a pick. His eyes meeting the steady ones of Peters, the Irishman stopped.

"I'm not after you," he said thickly. "It's that wall of coal that hems us in. I'm after chopping."

Peters listened, unmoved, to the approving murmur that came from the men. "Don't be fools!" he rapped. "One hefty swing at that stuff over there, and the rest of the mess will be down on us like a house!"

"Well," grunted the Irishman, "that's better than choking here, ain't it?"

"Is it?" sneered the foreman. "Who says we're going to choke, anyway? I say that a rescue party will be here long before our air gives out. They're probably on the way, this minute."

The Celt turned appealingly toward his fellows. "What do you all think?" he inquired angrily. "Do you want to take a chance and maybe die like men, or do you want to stay here and die like rats? Like rats, do you hear me? Rats!" His voice rose to a shriek.

"Pat's right," said one of the men resignedly. "Might as well get it over with."

"Oh, no you don't!" roared Peters. "Not while I'm foreman!" His voice softened. "Be reasonable, men," he pleaded. "Help will arrive, of that I'm sure."

"Blah!" jeered the Irishman. "What do the owners care about us miners? We're just a lot of trash to them." He spat noisily, by way of emphasis.

"You'll not do it, I tell you! You can't—!"

With a dull thud the Irishman's ham-like fist connected with the foreman's jaw, and the latter slumped to the floor, dazed.

A grimy little miner sprang to the blocked entrance, and with an exulting cry, drew back his pick for a mighty blow.

"Stop!" The cry came from Peters, who had raised himself to a sitting position. "Listen, men, *listen!*"

In the silence that ensued, all heard clearly a tapping sound, coming apparently from the roof. Three times it sounded and when Peters rapped heavily in response, the signal rang out again.

"You hear that?" cried the foreman exultantly. "The rescue party is here!" He drew out his watch and glanced at the radium dial. "Five twenty-five. We'll be out of here by six-thirty, I'll bet."

The men cheered lustily.

For half an hour, they heard no sound outside their anthracite prison. At six-five, by Peters' watch, the tapping was resumed. The men outside were working slowly and cautiously.

At length, when the air in the room had become so bad that the men were lying full length upon the hard floor, the point of a pick protruded suddenly from the roof, letting in a ray of light. In a few seconds it was withdrawn to allow a sweaty red face to peer in.

"Well, boys," said the wielder of the pick, "we'll have you outta here in a jiffy." And he was as good as his word.

As Peters stepped out of the coal dungeon where he had been imprisoned, he gripped firmly the grimy hand of his rescuer, and then slumped silently forward.

"I'm sure glad we got to you in time," said Bradley, the red-faced leader of the rescue party, who was speaking to Peters, as the latter lay comfortably upon a soft cot, sipping toddy luxuriously from a tall glass.

"It's darn lucky we heard your tapping when we did," amended Peters. "When we heard your picks at about five twenty-five, the men were just about to try and chop their way out the choked entrance. From what you say, they wouldn't have stood a ghost's chance with all that choke-damp in Gallery 2. But—" he broke off abruptly as Bradley gaped at him.

"You say that you heard us chopping at five twenty-five?" demanded Bradley in a puzzled tone.

"According to my watch that was about the time," said the bewildered foreman.

"Is your watch accurate?"

"Doesn't lose a second a year, I'll wager. What's the cross-examination about?"

"At five twenty-five," said Bradley slowly, "we hadn't even begun to dig. We were just making our way down Gallery 3. We couldn't have swung a pick until at least ten to six."

"Then who—?"

"Let me see your watch. I'll check it by the Bank's electric clock across the street." Bradley stepped to the window and peered out. When he returned, he said quietly, "Well, Peters, your watch was—"

And now, gentle reader, it's time for you to take a hand. All you have to do is to answer this question:

*Was Peters' Watch Right?*

# The Glass House Cure

Many, many years ago, there was a great king, who ruled over a large and prosperous land. This monarch was renowned for his wise and just laws, and people came from all over the world to live in his domains.

Now it chanced that in his kingdom was a criminal of the very worst caliber, who had for many years managed to evade the law. At length, however, the day arrived when the evil-featured murderer was brought up for trial before the king.

All the people waited with bated breath to hear what fate the ruler would allot to the super-criminal. Would he be hung, shot, burned or tortured to death? No one could tell, for the king's punishments were as erratic as they were just.

At last the news spread forth. The king had sentenced the criminal to live for the remainder of his days in a glass house. If he purchased so much as a single shade, his life would be forfeit. The astounded culprit, who had expected some terrible punishment, blurted out his thanks, but the monarch merely smiled wisely and said nothing.

Instantly a storm of protest arose from the people. The man was thoroughly bad, they cried. He certainly deserved death. What kind of a farcical punishment was this?

Many organizations sent formal protests, for the king had always invited comment from his people, but he remained adamant. Laughing within himself, the overjoyed criminal left for his glass house, which the king had ordered to be built at once in the center of a large and thriving town.

The moment the lawbreaker arrived, hot and dusty as he was, he was hustled through the transparent door into a luxuriously fitted parlor.

After a few curious glances about, he started to remove his collar and tie, which articles of apparel he had worn for the first time when he appeared before the king.

Even as his hand touched the necktie, however, he bethought himself, with a queer feeling, that his neck must be, without doubt, quite dirty. And as he saw the curious crowd outside, he stayed his hand. Could he allow this gaping mob of yokels to see that his neck was dirty? Never! Sighing, he released his grasp upon the tie, and dropping into a beautifully upholstered armchair, drew one arm across his sweaty forehead. A brown smear at once made itself apparent upon his wrist. My face must be awfully grimy, he thought. All at once he perceived two pretty country girls outside, staring at him and simpering. One of them touched her face illustratively. With a snort of disgust at his own lack of callousness, the hardened murderer hurried into the washroom, and for the first time in many days, scrubbed his hands and face.

Returning to the parlor, he again seated himself and placed his boots upon a dainty footstool, leaving a large dusty stain. Through an open window, he heard the following comment:

"How hardened that man must be. No appreciation of the beautiful things of life. Just look how he unfeelingly ruins a gorgeous bit of furniture! Would that I had it!"

With an angry snarl, the lawbreaker looked about him with the gaze of a trapped rat. Perceiving no way of escape, he strode again into the washroom and wiped and polished his boots, emerging with an angry glint in his eyes.

After sitting quietly for some time, he felt the gnawing pangs of hunger, and signaled for some food. In a short while, a lackey brought in a large platter heaped with delicious eatables.

Scarcely had the platter been deposited, when the criminal began to seize huge chunks in his fingers and worry them like a dog.

Immediately he heard a condemnatory murmur from the people outside, and abashed, he stopped eating. Then he noticed a knife and a fork beside his plate. Picking them up, he began clumsily to eat with them.

The crowd was again silent. He found himself forced to sip his liqueur daintily, and to refrain from drinking his coffee from the saucer.

The next day was similar to the first. Always under the eyes of the people of the town, a hitherto dormant self-respect came to life, and the criminal found himself obliged to be physically and mentally clean. He could no longer even read a Parisian magazine in peace. Each time he gazed at a picture, he could hear the people mutter, and with a sigh he would fling the lurid-covered thing aside, and take a book from "Doctor Eliot's Five Foot Shelf!"

At the end of ten years, he had become so famous, that men came from far and wide to observe the reformed criminal who had led such a pure and noble life. Constant reading of good literature had educated him to an amazing degree, and an essay of his entitled "Merits of Living in a Glass House," received worldwide acclaim.

And when the wise and just king was gathered to his maker, he appointed for his successor, none other than the man who had lived in a glass house. "For," said the king, "in his own mind, he will be living always in a glass house, and will bear himself accordingly."

# The Coward

Bob McNeil was a coward. He had always been a coward. From the time he had "licked dirt" in a vain attempt to escape a beating at the hands of the neighborhood bully, to his present contemptible part in this latest affair, he had been a spineless, worm-like creature.

McNeil was somewhat of a philosopher. He often wondered why a fate that had given him the body of a middleweight prizefighter in good condition had failed to endow it with even that bit of courage purported to be the standby of a cornered rat. But he never doubted that somehow, sometime, if the stress were great enough, he would forget his fear and play a hero's part.

But one more chance to redeem himself had passed by untaken, and as a result he was sitting miserably on the train watching familiar scenery slip rapidly by. No longer had he been able to stand the pointing fingers, the cutting whispers deliberately made audible.

"Yeah, that's him. A guy with a knife held up him and a girl. Hit the poor kid in the face, and McNeil didn't stir a finger. The yellow so-and-so!"

And the worst of it was, the whispering voices didn't lie. Sick with fear at the sight of the gleaming knife and the menacing glint in the man's eye, McNeil had readily, almost eagerly, turned his pockets inside out. And when the girl, a pretty, empty-headed thing, had made as if to scream, McNeil had remained motionless while the thug hit her brutally upon the jaw, knocking her sobbing to the ground.

What anger he felt at the sight had been overwhelmed in a great flood of fear that he might receive the same treatment. So he remained white-faced and trembling, even though the fellow contemptuously turned his back.

After that, he simply had to quit his job—he would have been invited to leave anyway, probably—and head for another town.

McNeil stared aimlessly out of the window, put aside the book he had been reading, and then allowed his glance to rove over his fellow passengers. Abruptly his eyes rested on a girl across the aisle a few seats ahead, and a warm flood of admiration swept over him.

Neatly dressed in a striking blue traveling ensemble, she was the most attractive girl he had ever seen. Lovely, vivid coloring, and a shapely, sensitive mouth rendered her face sweet and beautiful, and her eyes were dark and dancing as she drank in the rich green landscape. Probably her first long trip, mused McNeil.

As he stared at her in fascination, her eyes suddenly met his, and she smiled just a trifle before shifting her gaze. Unaware that people were watching, the delighted McNeil made frantic efforts to attract her attention again. Even as he succeeded, the world staggered madly, drunkenly about, the train seemed to drop and whirl, and there was a tremendous jarring crash that sent living flame along McNeil's neck, causing him to close his eyes in agony.

When he opened them a few moments later, the train was motionless, the shaken passengers were scrambling back to their seats, and two masked men with guns in their hands were coldly and malevolently surveying the scene.

Train robbers, who had derailed the train, was the thought that flashed into McNeil's brain. Covering the passengers with their weapons, they made their way down the aisle, glancing sharply at each female traveler. Then they stopped before the girl in blue and McNeil stiffened.

"This must be the one," growled the first man. "Blue traveling clothes, alligator bags, and everything. You're Senator Bingham's kid, ain't ya?"

"Of course she is," put in the second bandit, a shorter, thickset man. "There is no other girl like this one in the other cars."

The first robber seized the girl roughly by the arm. "We're after that string of emeralds you just got for your birthday, sister. Better hand them over."

The girl's face flamed defiantly. "I didn't bring them with me," she flashed out. "I'm not crazy!"

"Don't lie, you little fool! We know you have them with you."

"Stop fiddling with her," snapped his companion. "We ain't got all day."

Then it was that McNeil's blood boiled hot and acid in his veins, for the second bandit slapped the girl sharply across the mouth, leaving a thread of scarlet at one corner. With a little moan she surrendered her purse and the shorter man eagerly drew out a magnificent string of emeralds.

Why in heaven's name hadn't the little fool left them at home? McNeil wondered. And how could he even think of that now? Why, because he wasn't afraid, that's why. He was no coward. He was cool as ice. No he wasn't; he was red hot with flaming anger.

"My locket," the girl sobbed. "Please don't take that! It's a keepsake—" Her words were cut off as she cried out under a second brutal blow.

At this point, McNeil sprang to his feet.

Even as the first bandit's gun boomed, McNeil dove headmost in a splendid flying tackle that flung the man in a limp heap to the floor, his gun hurled spinning under the seats. Acting with miraculous speed and coordination that filled him with a glorious exaltation, McNeil leaped cat-like from the prostrate form of the first train robber and confronted his companion.

Rich, flaming courage seethed through his body, and disregarding the pointed gun he hurled himself straight at the man's throat. Searing pain ran through his chest as the gun spoke once, and again. Then his clenched fist connected in a mighty uppercut that split the heavy man's upper lip clear to the nostrils, knocked out all his front teeth, and sent him staggering back a full dozen paces to fall like a wet sack against the seats. And before the man could raise himself to a sitting position,

McNeil's fingers closed like a vice on his throat and held. Held despite the knifelike pain in his chest, held despite the powerful bandit's struggles, and closed ever tighter …

When he arose from the still form, McNeil wiped the blood from his fingers and faced the girl in blue. For a moment he stared at her stupidly. What did the hero always do when he had whipped the villains and saved the girl? Why, take her in his arms of course. But he didn't even know this girl. No matter; hadn't he fought for her? And wasn't there a warm look in her eyes?

McNeil drew her gently into his arms. For an instant he felt her lips on his, warm and sweet, and little lights in his brain flared red, yellow, and orange. Then he dropped plummet-like into a bottomless black void.

The coward was dead. His body, its neck broken by the derailed train's mad plunge into the rapids of White Water Gorge, lay crumpled next to that of the girl in blue.

# The Peasant Madonna

Antonio Cellini took the glittering little hypodermic in one trembling hand, inserted the extremely sharp point into the flesh of his arm, and pressing home the plunger, injected a quantity of colorless liquid. Then he seated himself in a rickety chair and waited for his quivering fingers to become steady.

In one corner of the little attic, where the dim light that struggled through the dirty window could strike it, stood an easel upon which rested a large canvas. The beautiful painting of a woman was complete in every detail save one. The woman had no face.

Antonio held up his fingers and gazed at them in a puzzled fashion. Fingers of a genius, they were, and had it not been for the mysterious nervous disease that caused them to tremble constantly, Antonio could have proved to a skeptical world his ability to paint.

But despite the heavy injection of cocaine, the long, slim fingers still shook perceptibly. Cellini buried his head in his arms in despair. Incurable, the first doctor had said, but another medical man, with an understanding look, had given Antonio his first injection. "That will fix you up," the doctor had assured him, a smile on his thin lips. And wonder of wonders, Antonio's hand had become as steady as steel. However, the effects had soon worn off, and Cellini found it necessary to take larger and larger doses. The doctor no longer smiled, but grimly demanded his money in advance, money that Antonio was at great pains to earn.

Antonio wanted madly to be able to finish his Madonna—his inspiration. The woman was not a well-groomed Madonna holding a chubby child, but a poorly dressed peasant woman, who held in hands that seemed to be trembling from cold, a thin, undernourished baby. But the beauty of the painting would lie in the Madonna's face—a face of infinite sweetness that would show a deep trust in God. And above her white hair, he would paint a misty, glorious halo.

Antonio wanted, above all things, to paint like Leonardo da Vinci, that immeasurably great genius, who had loved and made immortal Mona Lisa. How Leonardo had loved her! Antonio sighed.

And now, what could he do? Everything finished but the face, and the largest injection he had yet taken had proved to be of no help. His tortured nerves still sent frantic messages to his finger tips, and the latter twitched continually. Antonio was in despair. He had to finish her. He simply could not leave his Madonna thus. But perhaps tomorrow, his traitorous hands would remain steady.

Antonio undressed slowly and climbed wearily into bed. There he had an idea. He would pray to his ideal, Leonardo, to give him strength. "Just help me to finish my Madonna," he whispered. "After that—I don't care!" Presently, he slept.

That night Antonio had a vivid dream. He was trying desperately to fill in the face of his Madonna, but his hands shook so that he was afraid to put brush to canvas. Abruptly he felt a presence behind him and whirled about. Smiling sweetly at him, his brown eyes kindly, stood Leonardo da Vinci, just as the painter had envisioned him. Silently, the pleasant-featured genius took Antonio's brush. Holding the cheap thing by the extreme end, da Vinci began to paint. Such masterful, graceful strokes he made! The crudely made brush seemed to spring to life under his incredibly long, facile fingers, and the face of the Peasant Madonna began quickly to take form. Abruptly, Leonardo stopped, his fine eyes troubled.

"I—I don't know," he said slowly. "It seems that I can paint but one face, the face that has haunted me for many centuries. Perhaps you …" He passed the brush back to Cellini. The brush dropped from

Antonio's violently shaking hands and fell to the floor. With a sigh, da Vinci picked it up and resumed his painting. In a comparatively short time, the work was complete, but Antonio could not see it clearly, blurred as his eyes were with tears. With a last gentle smile, Leonardo disappeared.

Antonio Cellini awoke suddenly, and as he reeled, clutched for support, grasping his easel. He was standing before his painting. How he had come there, he did not know, but instinctively his eyes flashed to the face, and he paled.

"No," he muttered hoarsely, rubbing his eyes. "It can't be!" Hurriedly he flew over to a desk, and searching rapidly through the drawers, drew out a book of reproductions. With nervous hands he flipped the pages. At length he found what he was looking for. "Works of the Great Italians of the Sixteenth Century—da Vinci." Yes, it was so. That patrician face, that mocking, inscrutable smile.

"The only face he knew!" exclaimed Antonio thickly. For the face of the Peasant Madonna was that of Mona Lisa Giaconda.

Antonio's drugged body failed him suddenly, and he slumped abruptly to the floor. Mona Lisa, from her canvas, seemed to regard him silently, and it may be that the smile that captivated the ancient and modern world, deepened and grew tender, as she gazed upon the still form of Antonio Cellini.

# Seaside Flirtation

It must have been the singing that had broken his slumber, for that was the first thing he noted on awakening. Where the devil was he anyway? The snowy sand, sprinkled along the shore with great clusters of ragged grey rocks, brought sudden recollection; this was the secret little cove he'd been so delighted to discover toward the end of the long walk from his summer home.

The singing continued; the voice was fresh and clear, with the joyous lilt that indicates complete freedom from all responsibility. Irwin rose to his feet, stretched luxuriously, and frowned at the thought of the lonely return trip. A pearly cadenza leading easily into a ripple of notes that would have done credit to any coloratura who ever graced the Metropolitan, sharpened his lagging attention.

But in the name of Heaven, what language was that? Faintly suggestive of Castilian Spanish in their liquid cadences, the phrases were entirely foreign, even to a cosmopolite like Irwin Harding, who took pride in his ability to make himself understood—with tortuous gestures, of course—in almost any civilized country on the globe.

Certainly the matter merited an investigation; if the singer were as young and attractive as her voice, it might be worthwhile to induce her to beguile his time during the return home.

She must be behind that chest-high ledge of weed-grown rock, just lapped by the outer sea foam. As he approached, feet crunching the dry, white sand, he heard a little gurgle of dismay, and a startled face framed in long, lustrous hair appeared over the top of the ledge.

Irwin paused immediately, removed his cap, and as a concession to the girl's possible foreign origin bowed slightly. The doubt in her eyes was replaced first by reassurance, and finally by warm approval as she observed his good-humored eyes, crisp brown hair, and pleasant mouth.

Irwin's expression indicated even more unqualified appreciation. After a boring week at the seashore in the company of people notable only for their intolerable sameness, the discovery of a more than pretty girl with sea-green eyes, radiant unconfined hair, and a piquant mouth devoid of lipstick, was something of a welcome surprise.

"I—I beg your pardon," he began hesitantly. "I heard you singing, and naturally I was a bit curious. I wondered who had invaded my … um … domain. I hope I didn't frighten you."

Those unbelievable green eyes twinkled, but the girl remained silent.

"So you won't talk, eh?" smiled Irwin. "Well, I think I know why, young lady. You don't understand me, do you? I'm darned if I can place that language you were warbling in, but perhaps you know one of mine. Hmm … *Parlez-vous francais? … Non? … Habla* … er … *espanol*, or something?"

A flood of lilting syllables resulted as she laughingly mocked his painful linguistic efforts. Irwin smiled. He couldn't help it; she was as refreshing in her carefree joy as a cool drink after a five-set tennis match in the blazing sun.

"I'm coming over to your side of the fence," he announced hopefully, and started to round the ledge that separated them. Instantly the girl's mouth flew open in vigorous protest, and she gestured toward the part of her body hidden from his eager gaze. Her motion allowed him a breathtaking glimpse of lovely, bare shoulders.

He chuckled understandingly. "Don't tell me you tried to take a dip here?" he queried in a tone midway between concern and amusement, choosing to disregard her apparent ignorance of English. "Why, the surf's like a machine gun, and the undertow would drown a seal! No wonder you lost part of your swim suit, or are you missing all of it, my pretty maid?" He reflected for a moment, beneath her smiling glances, and came to a reckless decision.

"Listen, Princess," he blurted. "I'll give you such of my stylish apparel as I can in decency spare, and you do a Mrs. Tarzan act. Then, if you can overcome the remnants of your maidenly modesty, I'll be honored to escort you to the summer cottage of Harding, Senior, where his housekeeper can deck you out in one of my sister's Paris creations. Sis will love that! What do you say, honey? Please stop playing no talky; you've had your little joke."

But her oddly glowing green eyes still rested upon him with no sign of comprehension in their lambent depths.

With a resigned shrug, Irwin removed his shirt and tossed it to the girl. She caught it deftly, smiled her thanks, and in lieu of draping it about her, she smoothed the fabric with slim, water-wrinkled fingers, gurgling delightedly at the fine texture of the silk.

"Just like a woman," he reproved her teasingly.

Abruptly a hoarse shout reached their ears from the sea behind the girl, and dropping the garment she whirled with a little cry. Instantly Irwin seized the rock ledge and vaulted over simultaneously with her superb dive into the raging surf. He landed lightly upon his toes, but his knees buckled nevertheless, and he stared incredulously at the water.

It was not alone the girl's weird companion with his sickly-pale man's face framed in matted green hair that made him doubt his senses. No, it wasn't only that, for before she had disappeared beneath the waves, Irwin had seen the setting sun flash spectral colors on iridescent scales, and had glimpsed water frothing under the graceful beat of her filmy, green tail.

# Pierre Renard's Christmas

It was Christmas Eve. Inside the tiny cabin, despite the fiercely blazing logs, the temperature crept inexorably down. The Great Cold held the North in a grip of frosty steel. Never in the history of the region had it been so cold. Only the great white owl, in whose veins the leaping blood ran many degrees hotter than any man's, braved the still, deadly air in a vain search for food.

Pierre Renard stared hopelessly through the little window and cursed for the thousandth time the grim North and all those foolish enough to make homes there. The stertorous sound of Jeanne's breathing reached his ears above the snap and crackle of the flaming logs. Little Jeanne—fighting desperately against choking diphtheria for a life scarcely begun. Fighting almost without a chance, for the serum necessary to drive away that fatal grey membrane from her throat lay at Bitter Creek—forty-three miles away.

Forty-three miles! With the temperature close to seventy below, and dropping every hour! No man wise to the ways of the North ever traveled alone when the thermometer showed forty below. The clear, frigid air seared lungs like white-hot metal; no fur nosepiece could warm it; no warm-blooded creature could successfully combat it for long.

Pierre reflected bitterly. Christmas Eve! This was indeed a happy time. He had hoped that some of the boys from Bitter Creek would brave the week-old cold to look in on him. They knew he was here with Jeanne. Maybe Doc or Ed might show up yet; travel was slow in such weather. No, it was impossible. Forty-three miles! Jeanne was doomed.

He strode over to the bed and looked down at her. The blue eyes opened, and a smile trembled on her pale lips. Then she closed her eyes and resumed her labored breathing. Pierre's stolidity, born of many years' battle with relentless nature, broke completely. He bowed his head to the coverlet and wept. First Jeanne's mother—the gay, impulsive Marie—and now Jeanne ...

Abruptly Pierre stiffened. The sound of tinkling bells rang in his ears. Surely it was a dog-team from Bitter Creek. He might have known that Doc and Ed wouldn't let him down. Pray God they had some serum ... but how could they? They didn't know.

The door swung open to admit a freezing blast of air. Pierre stared in amazement at the man upon the threshold. Little Jeanne's blue eyes widened until they assumed the aspect of delft saucers. It was Santa Claus! He closed the door behind him and with many a heave and grunt overturned a huge sack upon the floor. An immense rainbow of objects flowed like a miniature river across the rough planks. Santa grinned approvingly at little Jeanne and nodded.

"Merry Christmas, Jeanne and Pierre," he rumbled in a deep, mellow voice. "There's medicine for Jeanne, and a few trinkets for both of you. Now I have to leave; it's getting late." Pierre vainly attempted to clear his fogged brain. Who was this masquerader from Bitter Creek? Couldn't be Doc; he was too small, and Ed would make two of this fellow. Before the puzzled Renard could find his tongue, Santa flung the door open, roared out a jovial "Brr-rrr!" and was gone.

Immediately Renard clutched his parka and gloves, and leaped for the door, muttering in bewilderment, "How did they know Jeanne was sick? How could they know?"

As he stepped out into the frosty night his ears were again assailed by the distant tinkle of sleigh-bells, but no dog-team was in sight. With the instinct of a trained trapper Pierre examined the snow. With growing wonder he followed the trail of tiny cleft hoofs to a little clearing. There it ceased abruptly, and on all sides stretched the pure Christmas snow unmarked.

# The True Story of Hercules

"What a husky little he-man he is!" said Hercules' father when the child was born. Zeus tended to be alliterative no matter what the occasion. Hercules' mother said nothing. That is she said nothing intelligible, but merely pressed the baby to her and cooed to it in what she mistakenly fancied to be its own tongue. But there was none of that quiet determination about Hercules as early as this. He squirmed and struggled, punctuated his wild swings with equally wild howls, and was only overcome by his father himself. And when it takes two adults to overcome a five-minute-old baby, you may be sure he will be quite a man.

Now as everybody knows, Zeus, King of Heaven, was Hercules' father, and since the child's mother was married to another man, Zeus would have found himself in serious trouble had he not been immortal. But as things were he had little to fear. One cannot poison an immortal husband, nor can one obtain a divorce when one is married to an absolute monarch. Juno, the wife of Zeus, was therefore forced to sit quietly in her favorite corner of the great Palace of Heaven and pretend that nothing was amiss between her and her mighty mate. And Juno had a long memory.

Thus it was that Hercules, through no fault of his own, acquired a powerful enemy the moment his birth became known. And while it is well to be son to the Lord of Heaven, it is not very well to be hated by his queen.

Hercules, historians tell us, was a strong and intelligent baby. His intelligence seems to have been overshadowed by his great strength, but it was there nevertheless. In proof of this, Aristogenes, one of the sources of the biography, cites a case in which Hercules showed taste and discrimination far beyond his years. When Zeus, who fancied himself the possessor of a most noble bass voice, would try to sing Hercules to sleep, the child would seize his royal father by the throat and refuse to relax his grip until overcome by Mercury, Apollo, and Diana the Huntress. He showed similar keenness of perception when on one occasion he set upon two gushing goddesses with his bottle and drove them screaming in terror from the nursery.

It was about this time that Juno's hate for Hercules overcame her natural love of children. Through bribing the curator of the Heavenly Museum of Arts and Sciences she acquired two great water snakes. These animals were by no means in a happy mood inasmuch as the museum was not well supplied with funds. Creatures who can go without eating for two or three months at a time are naturally exploited by scrimping curators.

And so, late that night the Queen of Heaven and fifteen or twenty demigods pushed the two vicious snakes through the open nursery door, closed it, and sprinted for their respective rooms. That is, all but Juno; she seated herself outside to enjoy the show. Presently she heard an odd childish cry and then sounds indicative of a struggle. There ensued then strange snapping noises which puzzled Juno. "Do snakes smack their lips over a good meal?" she wondered. Her curiosity being greater than her fear of the reptiles, she opened the door a trifle, peered in, and then staggered back, a spirit-broken woman.

Seated smilingly upon the floor was Hercules, joyously stretching the giant water snakes in and out like immense rubber bands! With a muffled sob of defeat, Juno fled to her room.

A few years later we find Hercules, an intelligent boy of eleven, under the care of one Cheiron, a centaur. Now a centaur is a reincarnated racetrack tout, and Zeus had contacted this one at Epsom Downs, where he spent much of his time. Cheiron, who had unblushingly professed himself an expert in mathematics, science, literature, mares, and contract bridge, took over, at Zeus' invitation, the task of instructing the youthful Hercules. As Cheiron fancied himself a mathematician without peer, he delighted in giving Hercules problems far beyond the boy's ability. One incident concerning such a problem is recorded by Aristogenes as an example of the first appearance in Hercules of that quiet perseverance and determination that was later to make his name anathema to every monster in Greece—and not a few in Peoria.

It seems that Cheiron, who had in some mysterious way acquired an elementary algebra book dated 1918, gave Hercules the following problem to solve, allowing him five minutes in which to arrive at a solution:

"There are a certain number of trees in an orchard. If the God of the Winds blows down three, and the farmer chops down half of those remaining, leaving six standing, how many were there originally?"

After wasting three of the five allotted minutes in gazing despairingly at the Table of Contents of the book, Hercules deliberately, and with malice aforethought entered farmer Socrates' orchard. After pushing over a certain number of trees, and an indeterminate number of protesting farmhands, he returned to Cheiron with the correct answer. Needless to say, future problems concerned themselves with objects too large for the boy to solve bodily.

Hercules, despite Juno's frantic preventive measures, had now arrived at the age of twelve, and his father, after some hesitation gave him into the hands of one Eurystheus to train further. Eurystheus was a real martinet, and assigned to Hercules twelve tasks, or labors, that would have made the single-handed capture of the Rock of Gibraltar in broad daylight appear an easy feat. These labors are doubtless familiar to you all, so I shall discuss only the more important of them, which are after all the ones that give us an insight into Hercules' character.

There was, in the Garden of the Hesperides, a tree that bore golden apples. The tree was guarded most efficiently by a giant dragon who was in a perpetually vicious mood due to a combination of insomnia and indigestion. The insomnia was caused by a nagging mother-in-law, and the indigestion by golden apples which can trouble even a dragon's digestive system. However, as Hercules was a more-or-less stubborn youth, he was determined to obtain both the apples, and an impromptu lesson in zoology; the latter to be acquired after a thorough if unprofessional dismemberment of the dragon and all his relatives, including the mother-in-law.

We see him now, clad in the skin of a great lion, striding swiftly through the unexplored forest, a heavy club in his firm grasp, keen brown eyes scanning the underbrush for possible danger, and his thick, yellow hair dangling unconfined over his muscular shoulders.

On the way to the Garden of the Hesperides he had many adventures, but we have no time to tell of them here. Aristogenes recounts with much gusto Hercules' encounter with Atlas, but we modern historians are forced to disbelieve the whole tale. It *is* true, however, that he exterminated a certain giant who had the inhospitable habit of utilizing cold steel in an attempt to render his visitors and his bed equal in length. As one cannot cut a bed to fit with a butcher knife, he used the instrument upon the guests, much to their dismay and acute discomfort. When Hercules left that neighborhood, a few of the giant's cronies were able—without any difficulty—to collect his remains in a cigar box.

Upon arriving at the garden, Hercules peered eagerly over the wall, and spying the dragon, thumbed his nose at it. The following conversation is said to have ensued:

The Dragon (In a rumbling bass voice): What do you here, rash mortal?

Hercules (Unperturbed, his eyes twinkling): I intend to do *you*, unless we can come to terms!

The Dragon (Somewhat uneasily): T-terms?

Hercules (Decisively): I'm not greedy. A bushel or two of golden apples is all *I* ask!

The Dragon (Dryly): What do you think this is, a fruit store? We've only one tree here and it bears but three apples yearly.

Hercules (Sighing): I guess I'll have to have this year's crop, then.

The Dragon (Rearing himself to his full one hundred foot height and flexing his muscles): Oh, indeed!

Hercules (His jaw set): So you want to fight, do you? Have at you then! (He springs lithely over the wall, club in hand)

The Dragon (Feebly): Y-you really want to fight?

Hercules (Calmly): Of course. I haven't had a good fight since I cleaned up a herd of tigers and made myself a full dress suit!

The Dragon (Slumping weakly to the earth): Well, strike me pink! I've been guarding this tree for some three hundred odd years, and nobody has ever so much as argued with me before. Why, why ... I don't know what to do. Hang on like a good fellow, will you, while I ring up headquarters?

Hercules (Firmly): Not a chance. I came for apples, and apples I'll have!

The Dragon (With something suspiciously like a sob): Oh all right, go ahead then, but I'll be docked—I just know it!

The foregoing conversation is vouched for by that great scholar Francis Bacon, and his collaborator, Lord Egg, so I do not hesitate to swear to its verity.

Eurystheus was much pleased with the success of Hercules' venture, and assigned to the youth the last and most dangerous labor—the bringing up from the underworld of the terrible three-headed dog, Cerberus. Hercules is said to have stated that he would rather wait until he died and save the journey, but that tale has been traced to Charles A. Beard, who has done much to discredit Hercules' reputation.

Cramming his meager belongings into a valise made from the skins of twelve great alligators, which he exterminated after a rousing fight in their own den, Hercules set out on the long dreary journey to the river Styx. The crooked path led often through dank, gloomy swamps and skirted yawning chasms, but Hercules' confidence never deserted him. After the creatures he had vanquished in fair or unfair fight, there was little that could disturb his equanimity.

Presently he arrived at the great black stream. The boatman regarded him in blank dismay.

"Are *you* dead?" he queried unbelievingly.

"Never was any deader," rejoined Hercules cheerfully, and with not a little sincerity, for he was tired from the long journey.

"Well," sighed the boatman, "I guess I'll have to take you across then. You might think I'd be relieved from night duty occasionally so that I could step out, but Pluto is an awful slave driver. I ain't seen a moving picture for weeks! Oh, well. Hop in."

"I don't think much of the view here," complained Hercules, straining his eyes into the darkness.

"You didn't come for the view, I hope," said the boatman dryly as he guided the boat dexterously past a few eagerly clutching disembodied spirits.

"What do those creatures want?" demanded Hercules a bit anxiously, as cold white fingers brushed his arm.

"They want to get in," said the boatman in an aggrieved tone, "but they ain't got the fare. We don't run this line for bums!"

"Fare?" asked Hercules nonchalantly, his hands digging desperately into the pockets of his lion skin.

"You heard me," said the boatman flatly. "We're in the hands of the receiver now because our fare is too low."

"Well, how much is it?" burst out Hercules.

"Oh, we ain't got no definite fare. That's the trouble. I wanted to charge one eye; Pluto, he held out for an index finger, and Persephone, our main stockholder, thought an ear or two would be about right," said the boatman carelessly as he slapped viciously at a daring spirit who had seized the end of the oar.

Then Hercules did the bravest act of his life. Without a word he dove over the side of the boat, and plunging deep into the icy black waters struck out for the low-lying shore of Hades. No one knows how he managed to make it; the waters of the Styx are as cold as the hands of the dead, and sap a man's strength like powerful drugs. But the fact remains that Hercules did make it, and if I seem prejudiced in my attitude toward this demigod, it is only natural admiration for a truly brave man.

Cold and tired, Hercules drew himself out of the water. In the distance he could see the walls of Hades, and there came to his ears the mournful and menacing baying of a great hound.

Clutching his heavy club, Hercules, without partaking of food or rest, set out for the walled city. Upon arriving at the great walls, he stopped for a breathing spell, and then prepared to scale them. Removing his lion skin he tore it into tough strips which he joined together to make a long rope. Making a noose in one end, he fastened a stone within it, and retaining the other end in his grasp hurled stone and noose over the wall. The first attempt was a failure; the stone did not catch, but on the second trial it did, and Hercules clambered easily to the top of the barrier.

With some surprise he found himself staring directly into a magnificently furnished palace. Through the window he could see a regal-looking man, whom he instinctively knew to be Pluto himself. Pluto was arguing very bitterly with a richly clad, beautiful woman. "That must be Persephone," thought Hercules, as their raised voices reached his ears.

"I won't do it, I tell you!" stormed Pluto.

"I think you will," said his wife icily.

Pluto kicked a heavy chair viciously across the room and tore his hair. "I will not!" he roared.

"Someone must take Cerberus out," said Mrs. Pluto calmly, "and I refuse to trust the poor creature to anyone else."

"Trust him? Trust that man-eater to anyone else? I wouldn't trust anyone else with him! Why ... why you're crazy, that's what you are!"

"John!"

"Oh, I don't mean that. Forget it. I'll take the damn creature out!" Snatching up a chain, Pluto strode from the room.

Hercules gazed thoughtfully at the woman for a moment and then snapped his fingers. Down the wall he went and stood outside the great gate. Presently Pluto, an angry look on his face, emerged, leading a monstrous three-headed dog.

At the sight of Hercules the dog gave a jerk at his leash that almost broke Pluto's wrist. "Lie down, you vicious brute!" snapped the King. "Who in the—! Who are *you*?" This last to Hercules.

"I," said Hercules cooly, "am a dog fancier, and just now I fancy yon tri-cephalic Whiffle-hound of yours."

"Y-you mean," asked Pluto fearfully, "you mean you actually *want* the confounded creature?"

"I do."

"Then for the love of heaven, take him and beat it! I've been trying to get rid of the brute for six hundred years. Why did I ever steal Persephone from her ma? Oh me!"

And thus Hercules completed the twelfth and last labor.

## II

"Where in heaven's name is Hercules?" roared Zeus, rising from his throne and shoving it angrily away from him. "It's twenty minutes after six!"

"Looks like he's late again," drawled Diana, "and after I went to the trouble to shoot a fine deer too."

"Plague take Hercules and the deer also! That fellow has kept me waiting for my dinner three times this week. A fine state of affairs." Zeus hurled a thunderbolt viciously at a passing comet, causing that unoffending body to dodge wildly to one side.

At that moment Apollo entered, flushed from his long and exhilarating gallop across the heavens. At the sight of the crowded table his eyes widened. "Don't tell me you've kept dinner for me?" he queried. "You know I can't make it on time."

"We're not waiting for *you*," snapped Mercury, his eyes fixed longingly upon a smoking cut of venison. "It's that inconsiderate Hercules. Went out dragon hunting again this morning, and is late as usual. You'd think he'd have exterminated every dragon in Greece by now."

"When he does," mused Diana, "I suppose he'll start on the iguanas."

"Is someone taking my name in vain?" demanded a cheery voice, and into the room strode Hercules. His massive chest rose and fell with his quickened breathing and a great welt marked one thigh.

"You're getting soft," sneered Cupid from his highchair. "You're all out of breath just from running upstairs."

"Running upstairs nothing!" snapped Hercules. "I just wiped out a family of fire-breathing dragons. I caught them out on a picnic. The old man sure put up a noble battle."

"Why must you persist in being so slangy?" protested the youngest of the Three Graces, who fancied herself a grammarian. "Can't you tell about your adventures in correct English?"

"One doesn't acquire refinement by associating with dragons and similarly ill-bred creatures," said Venus softly. "And that's what I like about Hercules—his virility and manhood." The fawn-eyed goddess smiled at him sweetly.

"Nevertheless," broke in the Grace, "I don't see why he doesn't kill a refined creature occasionally, instead of those horrid, badly raised dragons and hydras."

"Disregardful of the refinement question," broke in Zeus in his mighty bass voice, "I can't have you holding up my dinner every day. I think it's time you went on another labor."

"Another labor? So soon? Why, I just brought back the deer with the brass horns two weeks ago."

"That's two weeks too many for me. And besides I've a prayer here from the King of Crete. He says that there's some creature with six pairs of legs who's ruining business in his domain."

"Ruining business? How?"

"The boorish thing has flatly refused to patronize the local shoemakers and has started a barefoot fad. The loss has hit the shoemakers hard; after all, he's got six pairs of legs himself."

"I'm afraid you can't arrest him for that," commented Hercules dryly.

"I'm not arresting him because he's got six pairs of legs," bellowed Zeus. "I'm arresting him for not wearing shoes. It's unsanitary, dangerous, and borders on the indecent!"

"Di here does a good deal of her hunting barefoot," commented Hercules innocently, whereat that goddess blushed to the tips of her rosy ears.

"Don't compare a miserable six-legged subversive influence to a goddess!" snapped Zeus. "And anyway, I refuse to discuss the matter. The King of Crete has sacrificed twenty-three goats and a Persian to me this week, and I must do something. Go and get that human hexapod and bring him in—alive."

"Righto, but first I must taste a piece of that delicious deer meat."

"Delicious deer meat," muttered Mercury. "If Di hadn't shot that deer the creature could have got a pension from the government."

"Now I like that!" protested Diana. "I had to chase that deer through six miles of thorn-bushes in order to get a shot at it, and then the inconsiderate brute was only wounded."

"Enough!" cried Zeus, reaching threateningly for a thunderbolt. "I'll have no squabbling at the table!"

A strained silence ensued which was finally broken by Hercules.

"Well, I'm going," he said. "Where did the maid put my lion skin and my dragon-club?"

"They're in with your tennis racquet and golf clubs," said Venus with a simper.

"I'm off then. Goodbye, folks. I'll be back with the Shoemaker's Enemy in a month or so. Ta-ta!" And Hercules walked out.

Hercules had gone but a few feet into the forest when someone called his name. There stood Diana smiling at him wistfully.

"Hercules," she called breathlessly, "I want to ask you something."

"Well, do it quickly then; I've a long journey."

"Hercules, may I come along?"

"Come along?"

"Yes, I'm tired of hunting deer and lions; I want a chance at some big game. It must be glorious to conquer a great dragon."

"Is that the only reason?"

"Not exactly. You see, I'm getting thoroughly disgusted with things at home. Zeus' after-dinner stories are becoming terribly uninspired, and Mercury's table manners are atrocious. Ever since we allowed him to eat with us instead of waiting upon us, he's become quite obnoxious. Why, he and the Three Graces carry on in a most scandalous manner!"

"Well … I don't think much of a woman as a dragon hunter, but run back and pick up a bow and a quiver of arrows and come along.

After all, this six-legged creature is not as dangerous as an ogre or a dragon."

"Hercules, you're a brick!" And Diana sprinted lithely back to the palace to return shortly with a hunting bow and a quiver of long, deadly arrows.

Although Hercules had done much to render this part of the forest safe for travelers, there were still not a few dangerous animals in its depths. And the meeting of Hercules and Diana with one of them makes a tale that causes Jovian laughter to echo across the great Table of the Gods to this day.

Now it chanced that near the path the two were following, lived an immense dragon who claimed to be able to trace his ancestry back to the Garden of Eden. As Hercules and Diana passed within a few feet of his den, talking in recklessly loud tones, the dragon emerged, regarded them in a puzzled fashion as if wondering which to exterminate first, and then charged, his ponderous many-ton bulk approaching them with the speed of an express train.

Diana uttered a little cry and fumbled for an arrow, but Hercules promptly shoved her spinning into the underbrush and faced the monster alone, club in hand. The dragon almost stopped in sheer amazement at the sight, and then apparently recollecting what must inevitably become of his reputation if he hesitated now, resumed his charge. A full hundred and ninety-nine feet he towered above Hercules, and with a sulphurous sneer he raised a clawed forefoot to crush out the demigod's life. At that moment a feathered shaft appeared in his scaly breast and then another. For a heartbeat the monster stood there, his menacing paw raised, before sinking back upon his haunches. The murderous and ferocious expression upon his scrambled features was replaced by one of love and understanding. He then seized Hercules gently by one ear and proceeded to lick him thoroughly and affectionately with a seven-foot barbed wire tongue.

He had just about reduced Hercules' torso to the color of a raw carrot, when Diana emerged from the bushes, her face scratched and bleeding. Placing her small hands upon the dragon's side she shoved him away, allowing the much bewildered Hercules to get to his feet. In answer to the unspoken question in his eyes Diana laughed a trifle hysterically and explained: "It's that little rascal Cupid, God bless him. He's forever mixing his arrows with mine."

Aristogenes is inclined to belittle Hercules' part in this "battle," but the other historians and myself have agreed after much research that Hercules was not yet out of the conflict when Diana loosed her shafts.

Presently the two arrived at Crete and set out in search of the six-legged terror whose name they found to be Geryon. They found him in a most unexpected manner. One day while going through the woods, Hercules and Diana heard the sound of bitter sobbing. Upon peering about the bush from which the weeping emanated, they perceived a sorry-looking creature in the semblance of a large man, mightily muscled, with six pairs of legs. Most of them were bare, and a few were bound with bloodstained rags. There he sat, rocking himself to and fro and moaning in a heartbroken fashion. When Hercules tapped him on the shoulder, he sprang up nervously with a little cry. Then he sighed and sat down again.

"I thought it was the shoemakers coming back," he said in a choked voice. "I thought they had relented."

"You are Geryon?" queried Hercules.

"I am that poor creature. Oh, my feet!"

"I understand that you have broken the law. I must put you under arrest."

"Broken the law?" The creature stood up. "It's a lie!" he cried.

"Haven't you refused to patronize the local shoemakers?"

"What? Refuse to patronize them? Why, they won't sell me any shoes. I've been on my knees to them, but on the King's orders they will not sell me any footwear at all. Not even slippers."

"Why in heaven's name should the King do that? Why, he said—"

"Never mind what he says. He's mad at me, that's what. Last year," he sobbed, "at the Royal Soccer Tourney I defeated his All-Star Team single-handed, and he's never forgotten it. Boo-hoo!"

Hercules looked questioningly at Diana. There were tears in her fine eyes.

"I think," said the demigod slowly, "that our expedition was a failure, Diana. Let's go."

And they strode away leaving Geryon to sob in safety in the bushes. Which shows, I think, that Hercules was not the muscle-bound, soulless creature some biographers would have him.

# The Tooth

Richard McAllister exclaimed softly when he saw what his spade had struck in the garden loam. Wedged tightly between two tough roots it was a great yellow, pointed tooth. McAllister dropped instantly to his knees and began to twist it back and forth in an effort to release it. But it was only after cutting the entangling roots with a knife that the curious scientist was able to wrench the encrusted fang free.

The tooth was at least fifteen inches long and proportionately broad, and upon the tip, which had been forced deep into an iron-hard tree root, was a small round bulge. As to the anthropological value of his find, McAllister entertained not a single doubt, and he blessed the whim that had started him spading his garden this evening.

After taking the specimen into his cottage, McAllister examined it minutely with the aid of a powerful magnifying glass and a pair of calipers. It resembled the tooth of any large reptile except as to proportions, but the bulging tip filled the anthropologist with wonderment. To what end a rounded tip on a tooth obviously designed for piercing? And that poison groove along the side; there were no large poisonous reptiles native to Greece even in prehistoric times.

Unwilling to leave such a precious biological discovery in his lightly-built cottage, McAllister returned to the garden, forced the great fang deep into the rich loam, tamped the earth firmly about it, and leaving all to the cold light of the moon went thoughtfully to bed.

McAllister awakened suddenly. It was very early; the sun was just reddening the sky. He wondered what had broken his slumber. Then he heard it—a sound as of someone pounding the earth, a ponderous heaving and jerking.

Throwing a light robe over his pajamas, McAllister flung open the front door and peered curiously about. What he saw stopped him dead in amazement. In the middle of the newly-spaded garden was a burnished helm topped by a nodding red plume. To the scientist's unspeakable horror and unbelief the helmet twisted to and fro with mighty, purposeful movement. And slowly a pair of metal-clad shoulders were pushing up through the soft earth—shoulders as broad as those of a giant.

Still paralyzed, McAllister saw the beams of the rising sun play dazzlingly upon the bright point of a great lance brandished by a gauntleted hand. Then with an herculean wrench, the immense form of an armored man freed itself from the clinging soil, and leaped lithely toward McAllister. Through the grillwork of the helmet the dazed anthropologist saw two gleaming eyes—eyes as soulless as those of the Devil himself.

Some fleeting thought of addressing the creature flitted momentarily through McAllister's mind, to be banished by the couching of the ten-foot, metal-shod lance.

With a choked cry of terror, McAllister swung the door shut and locked it. There was a splintering crash as the lance, flung by more-than-human strength, pierced the door like so much paper to bury one-third of its length in the wood and plaster of the wall opposite. It was still quivering violently as ten inches of keen sword blade slit the door from top to till. But McAllister had not waited; the open back door testified to his hurried departure toward the village and police.

The Magistrate of the little Greek village looked up in mild surprise, as Richard McAllister, whose Scotch-English aplomb had often evoked comment from his more volatile neighbors, burst into the office, one trembling hand clutching a flimsy robe about him.

"A madman!" gasped the scientist. "He dug a hole in my garden; he's dressed in outlandish armor, and he's got a sword about a mile long! He almost killed me!"

But when McAllister and three skeptical officials entered the garden it was deserted. Their skepticism was replaced by keen interest, however, when they were shown the giant lance, which their combined efforts failed to withdraw. As they made the usual inspection of the room, and were peering wonderingly at a great footprint, a sharp cry from McAllister brought them quickly back to the garden. They found him clutching a tooth—a tooth cracked neatly open at the tip to disclose a hollow interior.

The fang seemed to create an abnormal excitement on the part of the scientist, and the policemen eyed him curiously. At that moment there was a hoarse shout behind them and they whirled to see the armored madman himself bounding toward them. Hastily two of the officers fired. One missed completely; the other's bullet struck the light plate-armor at an angle and glanced off. Then the man was upon them. A two-handed sword sped in a glittering arc about his head, and a policeman fell decapitated to the ground. A second powerful stroke caught McAllister an indirect blow upon the head, and he wavered senseless to the earth. But not before he had glimpsed the effect of that stroke upon the other two men ...

When he recovered his senses, all three of the officers were dead or dying, and of the madman there was no sign. As a swarm of officials and curiosity-seekers poured like ants into the garden, McAllister greeted them with a hollow, eerie laugh.

"The Dragon's Tooth!" he shrieked. "The Dragon's Tooth of Cadmus! A-ha! Ha! Ha!"

# Return to Me

She took the V-mail letter from her sister without curiosity, even though it was the first in weeks. What was there to be curious or excited about? They were all the same, and each one seemed to sear her with its hastily scrawled lines.

She opened it under the contemptuous eyes of her kid sister, so righteous in the fierce idealism of eighteen. Yes, it was the same. "My darling Jeanne ..." and the usual positive affirmation of his faith in a love that no longer existed, if it ever had. And most ironic of all, the repetition of a phrase that appeared in so many of his letters: "Once again I have come through Hell, and I know it is because of the love that reaches me; a love almost tangible in its intensity. It's a little frightening at times."

She placed the letter wearily on the secretary, conscious still of the critical eyes of Marge.

"Well?" her sister demanded breathlessly. "Are you going to tell him about—about Dr. Grayson? It's not fair! It's mean and cruel!"

Jeanne looked at her coldly. How could she make it clear to a child of eighteen that people didn't often do wrong out of sheer devilry. They were helpless pawns in a net of forces only vaguely understood. She had believed in her love for Phil, but in the two long years he had been overseas, her faith had wavered. Was she to blame if she found the smooth, subtly ironic doctor so much more thrilling than the blunt, almost crude Phil, with his small-town philosophy and ignorance of the deep lying significance of things? Could she discuss with him the regal surge of Brahms, or the malicious humor of Saki?

It was all so clear, and yet, with her sister's bitter eyes upon her, she felt unaccountably guilty. Ought she to tell Phil? Of course, under ordinary circumstances she would do so as bravely as she might, but wasn't it better now to sustain him in the faith that underlay his magnificent battle courage? When he came home, then ...

She shuddered as she thought of his unshakable belief in their love. How mistaken a person could be, writing ecstatically of a great love, when all her mind and heart had, for months now, been the unique possession of a certain doctor with kind, laughing eyes. Self-hypnosis was the only explanation. In the muck and terror of battle, he had mesmerized himself into feeling a current of love that to his disordered imagination could span three thousand miles of water to wrap him in its beneficent warmth. Well, surely it was better that way. At least if it happened—he'd have that comfort, never knowing it was false.

Her musings came to an abrupt close with the jarring clamor of the doorbell. Marge left the room to answer it, and Jeanne felt less oppressed. Her own thoughts were bad enough, but that kid sister didn't help much in her self appointed role of gadfly.

Marge returned, white and breathless, clutching a telegram. Jeanne took it, almost with aversion. Was it—? No, it wasn't from the War Department. She ripped it open, conscious of her sister's warm breath as Marge peered tiptoe over her shoulder.

He was coming home for good! A thrill of dread ran through her. The crisis could no longer be shoved into the background of her mind. She turned to meet Marge's eyes, and seeing the golden fire in their depths, she knew all at once that it was no self hypnosis that warmed a man in a fox hole three thousand miles away.

Everything was going to be all right, now.

# The Surgical Cracksman
# and the Crime School

Doctor Godfrey van Nuys had just finished a late breakfast in the quiet
dining room of the exclusive Vesalius Club when the note was handed
to him by an attendant. He took it gently between his supple, surgeon's
fingers, and examined it thoughtfully as though he had some
knowledge of its contents. Then he ripped it open and scanned it with a
single quick glance. The merest suggestion of a frown touched his
slightly aquiline features.

"Any answer, Doctor van Nuys?" inquired the attendant.

Van Nuys shook his head and smiled ruefully. "I have grave
doubts that you could find the messenger now if you called out the
whole police force, Charles," he remarked grimly. "Thank you."

When the puzzled servant had padded away, the doctor read the
note once more. It was brief and very much to the point:

Doctor Godfrey van Nuys, the distinguished surgeon—alias the
Surgical Cracksman—is cordially invited to take the entrance
examinations for admission to the Crime School. Be at the corner
of Franklin and Pine tomorrow evening at eight—alone.

Van Nuys sighed. And he had so foolishly believed that outside of himself and his lovely and quick-witted accomplice, Gale LaSalle, nobody knew that the brilliant young surgeon was also the equally brilliant safecracker who invariably left within the empty strongbox a card reading—and meaning—precisely:

You may recover all your valuables by donating one thousand dollars to the Cancer Research Foundation.

- The Surgical Cracksman

There had been, of course, the possibility that the servant who had glimpsed his unmasked face on that hectic night a few weeks ago might have recognized the lithe prowler as the popular Doctor van Nuys. On the night in question, the Surgical Cracksman had outwitted a famous detective agency and the police to slip through a guarded estate with Lady Cynthia Leicester's diamond necklace. That servant, he felt sure now, was a member of the Crime School who was probably there for the same illegal purpose as van Nuys.

The young surgeon whistled softly. They had him fast. His fingerprints from that first amateurish job were still on file. Let the police grow suspicious through an anonymous tip, and he was finished. Public sentiment was high against the phantom safecracker who stole to benefit a cancer clinic—and for the love of adventure. No, Doctor van Nuys would have to make terms with the Crime School.

The Crime School! That almost legendary organization about which nothing was known save that it did exist and had successfully committed every profitable crime known to the underworld. Van Nuys shook his head gloomily. Obviously they wished to number him among their group.

He looked about him at the rich furnishings of the Vesalius Club, and chuckled despite his predicament. What would the members say if they knew that the Surgical Cracksman was a member in good standing? But this was no time for ironic musing. He must get in touch with Gale at once, and warn her. Perhaps her connection with him was not known to the Crime School.

The telephone was obviously not to be trusted for communication; they might have her wires and his tapped. Van Nuys strolled into the next room, found some stationery and wrote Gale a brief message explaining the situation and ordering her to keep under cover until she heard from him.

At precisely eight o'clock of the next evening, van Nuys paused casually at the corner designated, and glanced searchingly about. A few moments after the hour an unobtrusive car of a popular make pulled up beside him.

"Doctor van Nuys, I believe?" queried the driver, a grey-haired man who looked rather like a professor.

Van Nuys smiled a trifle wryly. "I'm your man," he said briefly, and opening the rear door, stepped in. To his surprise the back seat was already occupied by an exquisitely gowned young woman whose tiny mask only emphasized the perfection of red lips and dimpled chin. She turned to face him as the car accelerated smoothly.

"Director's orders," she said smilingly. "I'm to blindfold you." Van Nuys submitted wordlessly as she wrapped a filmy black scarf about his face and knotted it. The scarf smelled faintly of some exotic perfume.

"Now we can get acquainted," she said pleasantly, her voice low and rich. "My name is Moira, and I'm professor of blackmail at the Crime School."

The Surgical Cracksman could not help chuckling at her frankness. "Aren't you being rather confiding to a total stranger and, may I add, an enemy?"

She laughed, and the sound reminded him of the coughing purr of a tiger. "Not at all," she informed him coolly. "You see, you will either pass my tests and become one of us, or—" She paused significantly. "Need I say more?"

Godfrey's lips tightened. As a successful physician he knew human nature, and nothing was more certain than that this lovely, fragile girl was animated by an icy mind and possessed of an indomitable will. There was that in her tone that convinced the surgeon of her utter indifference to the code of civilized society.

But when he spoke, his voice was as casual as hers. "My dear, you make yourself perfectly clear," he said pleasantly. "I'm sure that you are a wonderfully effective professor."

She chuckled appreciatively, and the car purred on with no further conversation. Presently it slowed to a halt, but whether in town or miles away, van Nuys could not determine. They had certainly avoided the main traffic lanes, but that fact helped him little.

Moira slipped her warm hand into his, and they proceeded up thickly carpeted stairs, through a long corridor, and into a room that smelled faintly of antiseptics. There the blindfolded surgeon was paused momentarily before some device that hummed like a giant bee.

When the humming ceased, Moira led him through several adjoining chambers and finally released him in a room obviously already occupied. There the scarf was deftly untied and van Nuys found himself facing a masked man across a great desk.

"Please be seated," said the man courteously. "I'm the Director."

Silently van Nuys seated himself before the desk. Moira and the grey-haired chauffeur sank into chairs on either side of him. The men and women already in the room eyed the surgeon silently, and he felt like a man upon who sentence is soon to be pronounced. A burning desire to wreck this mocking complacency swept him. A disdainful smile touched his humorous lips, and turning deliberately in his chair he gazed searchingly at each person in the room. As his keen, contemptuous glance passed from a bald little man who looked like the proverbial henpecked husband, to an amazon-like woman apparently capable of fighting any three ordinary men, he spoke in biting, derisive tones.

"I've seen children play at secret societies of this kind," he said witheringly, "but for infantile attempts to create atmosphere you people are far superior. Why not drop the folderol and act like the business men and women your activities indicate you are."

The Director's grin gave the cue to the other members, and quiet smiles of amusement swept the room. Abruptly the man behind the desk became serious. He turned to Moira. "Mr. van Nuys is unarmed, I presume?"

She nodded. "Oh, yes; the doctor is very understanding."

Godfrey glanced questioningly at the Director, who regarded him with half concealed amusement.

"As you may find out, we are scientific here, doctor. You were stopped before an x-ray setup before being brought to this room. It would have detected even a thin scalpel taped, let us say, under your arm. The last medical man we attempted to make use of had such a surgical blade taped to the inside of his thigh … However, now to business." He rose to his feet. Van Nuys eyed him with curiosity; the Director had the build of an athlete, the tones of a cultured man.

"Doctor van Nuys," he began, "as you may know, we are a specialized group of criminals. Each of us, and we number thirty at present, is an expert on some subject pertaining to crime. Moira is an expert on blackmail. She has worked out a practical method for acquiring incriminating documents; her degree in psychology from a great German university has enabled her to perfect a psychological approach that never fails. Blackburn, your chauffeur tonight—he has an antipathy toward masks, Blackburn—is a mechanical genius who could run a twenty-year-old car on condensed milk. Incidentally, he can devise equipment to crack any safe ever built—which ought to interest you, doctor."

He paused momentarily, and van Nuys broke in. "With such a wonderful organization, what possible use can you have for me?"

The Director smiled. "You are the only medical man with real intelligence over whom we have a definite hold. Heretofore we have been compelled to try to employ dope peddlers and quacks. The attempts were all failures; they couldn't pass our rather rigid tests."

He noted the surgeon's unspoken question, and his gaze once more fell upon Moira. "In order to receive reasonable assurance that every member of the Crime School is possessed of more than ordinary brilliance of intellect," he continued, "we subject each recruit to three tests devised by our psychologist, Moira. Anybody who fails, no matter how willing he may be to serve us, would be a potential menace to the rest of the group." Again he paused, and van Nuys sensed the same icy quality in this man that characterized Moira. "Therefore, the failures are eliminated— as you might say in horror, murdered."

Van Nuys yawned and reached for a cigarette, almost chuckling aloud as he glimpsed the respect in the Director's eyes at this evidence of perfect coolness. Then the Director deliberately turned his back to the surgeon and whipped aside a pair of thick hangings behind his desk. Through the pane of clear glass thus revealed, van Nuys could see a haggard-faced man seated apprehensively upon a chair within an iron-walled little chamber.

"This doctor," the Director informed the Surgical Cracksman, "failed the first of our tests. I have waited to eliminate him in order to prove our sincerity to you. When I pull this lever a bomb of potassium cyanide will drop into a carboy of acid, releasing deadly prussic acid gas. It will be over very quickly. By the way, that is one-way glass; the victim cannot see us." And the Director, as though lecturing to a high school biology class, pulled the lever.

Despite his efforts to remain calm, the horrified surgeon bent forward in his chair. In the execution chamber the man sprang suddenly to his feet, clutched at his throat, and fell writhing to the floor.

"The body will be disposed of by our chemists," the Director said calmly, pulling the hangings together again. Van Nuys stared at him with such loathing that the Director appeared to color slightly.

Moira chuckled. "He has an amazing ability to make one feel inferior," she informed the Director, "but my tests will soon determine his real qualifications."

The execution concluded the interview, and Moira conducted van Nuys up to the room where he was to spend the night. At the door the girl paused deliberately. "You know," she said frankly, "I like you, Godfrey."

Van Nuys looked at her, and there was no attempt on his part to hide the dislike in his eyes. "I'm sorry I can't say the same about you," he told her coolly, and his smile could not remove the sting from the retort.

"You are very tactless, doctor," was Moira's low-toned answer. "You see, those are my tests you will take tomorrow." And she turned abruptly on her heel and left him.

Early the next morning the Surgical Cracksman was served a well-cooked breakfast and brought to the chamber where the first test was to take place. The situation, which at first had seemed merely melodramatic, had now become a highly serious matter. These criminals might be overly dramatic in their approach, but they left no doubt in his mind that there was a psychological reason behind every action. After all, the daily activities of people like these tended toward melodrama; where except in fiction could one expect to find a girl like Moira?

The preparations for the first examination were begun in a businesslike manner. Van Nuys was securely bound to a heavy chair in a darkened room.

The Director lingered to offer a few words of explanation. "In a moment," he told the Surgical Cracksman, "you will be confronted with a test of your ingenuity. If you cannot remove a certain menace to your life within one hour you will die, either from the test itself, or if you prefer to call out, the gas chamber." As he spoke he switched on the lights. "Look up, doctor."

Van Nuys did so and gasped. Suspended several feet above his head by a heavy rope was a great metal ball. A smoking fuse led to the supporting rope.

"That fuse will burn to the rope in exactly one hour," the Director informed him gravely. "In that time you must find the sole means of escaping the falling ball. Remember, if you prefer the gas chamber, just call out. Good luck, doctor; we need you badly." And the Director strode from the room.

Van Nuys stared up at the massy sphere and his heart beat faster. Then he began a careful survey of the contents of the room, of his bonds, and of the deadly fuse that sputtered many inches from his reach. His gaze returned to the ball, and abruptly his eyes narrowed …

Ten minutes after the commencement of the test, the Director responded to a vigorous hail from van Nuys. Viciously the Crime School head ground his cigarette beneath a heel, disregardful of the expensive rug. "Looks as though your doctor isn't what we thought he was," he remarked to Moira with a disappointed air. The girl paled slightly.

Doctor van Nuys greeted him with a cheerful smile as he entered the room. The Director regarded him almost pityingly. "You've given up rather quickly," he said.

Van Nuys chuckled. "I'm so sorry to have hurt your tender feelings," he said ironically, "but I have not given up. By the simple expedient of blowing vigorous breaths in the general direction of your cleverly contrived ball, I have proved to my satisfaction that it is a carefully painted sphere of some very light substance, perhaps a paper shell. Surely no metal sphere would quiver at a breath."

"Excellent!" The Director's tone was warm with admiration. "You will be released immediately for the next test. And may I tell you that I am the only other person to equal your time."

Van Nuys regarded him with a trace of contempt. "In bad company again," he sighed. "I guess I'll never learn."

After his release, van Nuys was further congratulated by other members of the Crime School. The irony of the situation amused him. He recalled the day he had passed his anatomy exams; at the time they seemed more important than the tests he was now undergoing.

Moira herself undertook to explain the next ordeal, under the watchful eyes of the Director and several others. "You will be locked in a room for two hours," she began. "In that room there are a certain number of objects. In order to pass the test you must name and place correctly eighty per cent of the objects. That's all there is to it—you know the price of failure." Van Nuys thought he detected a slight break in her voice as she turned away.

For two interminable hours the perspiring doctor concentrated his highly trained mind upon the bric-a-brac that cluttered the little room. When he was led out for the questioning, a horrible premonition that he had failed assailed him. The Director, a photograph of the test room before him, acted as the interrogator with a dispassionate manner that infuriated van Nuys. Slowly the toll mounted:

"One ashtray, south-east corner."

"Check."

"Two figurines—in very bad taste, too!—end table, west side."

"Check."

And so it went on.

At the end of twenty minutes van Nuys paused, his mind a complete blank.

The Director eyed him questioningly. "There are exactly one hundred objects in that room, doctor. You've named seventy-nine of them with passable accuracy. You need one more, and according to custom you're allowed ten percent of the time already used. Two minutes, Mr. Surgical Cracksman ..."

Desperately the surgeon attempted to re-picture the room. Surely he could hit upon one of the remaining twenty-one objects; he must. As the inexorable seconds raced by, his heart also raced. Some thought of a reckless leap at the Director flitted through his mind. Then Moira glanced casually at the spectators, yawned ostentatiously, and gazed as if in surprise at her tiny jeweled wristwatch.

"A clock, east wall!" snapped van Nuys.

The Director pushed aside his photograph and pad with a sigh. "Check, doctor, and my congratulations."

Once again Moira paused at van Nuys' door; the last test was scheduled for a few hours later.

"I suppose I ought to thank you," the Surgical Cracksman began somewhat ungraciously. "I would have been lost without that hint."

Moira stared at him in real or simulated wonder. "Are you implying that I gave you some sort of hint, Doctor van Nuys? If so, please disabuse yourself; there are no traitors in the Crime School." But van Nuys fancied he glimpsed a slight twinkle in her dark eyes before she turned to go.

As he rested upon the comfortable bed, the Surgical Cracksman mused upon the nature of the last test. It was success as much as failure that concerned him. He had no wish to join this organization. And there was Gale to be considered; they were to be married when he had "contributed" one hundred thousand dollars to the Cancer Research Foundation. No, if he passed the last test or not, the Surgical Cracksman had to break from this cunning snare.

To his surprise the last test proved to be one well suited to his talents; it was invariably a specialized test of the recruit's professional expertise.

Fifty miniature doors fitted with a variety of locks provided the last obstacle to van Nuys' becoming a member of the Crime School. Before the frankly admiring eyes of some twenty members, the Surgical Cracksman—with the aid of a complete kit of his own tools, all of which he had designed after some months' work in a safe factory during his med school years—succeeded in opening the little steel doors at an incredible rate.

A recent model lock with noiseless tumblers held him at bay for some moments, but a sensitive microphone pick-up proved its undoing.

"You are now a member in good standing," the Director informed him as the last of the safe doors swung open. "Congratulations."

"Which means exactly what?" demanded van Nuys challengingly.

"This. Moira has succeeded admirably in obtaining an almost ironclad will in her favor from Karl Richter, the millionaire—and one of your occasional patients. His health is not very good, and we should like him to die before he is persuaded by his overzealous relations to change the money distribution. Naturally there must be no suspicion of foul play or the will may be broken."

Van Nuys set his jaw; this was worse than anything he had expected. "If you think I'll be a party to the murder of one of my patients, you're crazy! I don't do things that way, so do your damnedest!"

The Director sighed. "I expected you to refuse—at first," he said blandly. "Moira, have them bring in Miss LaSalle."

"Gale!" gasped van Nuys.

"Yes, Gale; she was foolish enough to follow you here—or did you hope to deceive us with such a childish expedient?"

"Godfrey, darling!" Gale was flushed and panting as the guards led her in. "I'm sorry, Godfrey," she said penitently, meeting his glance. "I disobeyed your letter. I—I was worried about you."

The Director cut in smoothly. "Have you reconsidered, doctor?"

"What are you going to do with her?"

"If you join us, she becomes your assistant—and we'll waive the tests."

The Surgical Cracksman's mind raced. It was obvious that once he was no longer of immediate use to them both he and Gale would be killed. The Crime School knew the danger of unwilling members.

Then he smiled, and glanced significantly at Gale. "I suppose I have no choice," he said wryly, walking toward the desk.

"You're acting wisely," said the Director, rising with outstretched hand. Moira stood beside him, smiling.

Van Nuys seized the Director's hand and went into action. With a nervous strength that belied his slender build, he jerked the relaxed Director across the desk in a welter of papers and broken glass. His fist, impelled by all the force of a muscular right arm, drove crashing into the man's jaw. Simultaneously Gale broke from the light grip of her two guards and hurled the contents of her compact, held ready since van Nuys' cue, into the eyes of the guard at her right. As the pepper-blinded man pawed at his eyes, van Nuys leaped for the lever that released the gas in the iron-walled chamber. The other guard's shot flew wild as Gale flung her cape over his head, while van Nuys released the lever long enough to hurl a heavy inkwell through the pane of one-way glass. Strangely enough, Moira stood calmly against the wall, making no move to interfere.

As the almond-scented gas began to pour from the broken glass of the adjoining chamber, van Nuys leaped desperately for the door already opened by the quick-witted Gale. For an instant as he passed through, the Director had a clear shot at him, and there was death in his eyes.

But the bullet meant for the Surgical Cracksman buried itself in the fragile body of Moira, who had leaped to shield him. Dying she fell to the floor, and the door closed as Gale and the doctor hurled their combined weights against it.

They could not hold it long against three men, but time was unnecessary. In a few seconds all sound from within ceased. The deadly gas had done its work well.

It took but a few moments to make their hurried way out of the building, meeting nobody in the somber corridors. As they reached the street of a familiar residential section, van Nuys clutched at Gale's arm.

"We've got to get away, Gale; there are at least a few other members who know I'm the Cracksman. Darling, we won't wait for that hundredth donation; we'll get married by the captain of a ship—Captain Larsen. If we ask him, he'll keep us aboard his tramp steamer until he's ready to sail. We'll go far away, maybe to South America. Are you game, Gale, dear?"

She smiled tenderly. "Does it take a whole Crime School to get you to pop the question, Mr. Surgical Cracksman?" she asked jokingly. And then in a low voice, "I'll go anywhere in the world with you, sweetheart."

# A Dictator Dies

The Dictator was critically ill. The paralysis from which he was suffering was easily identified, but the surgeons knew of no effective treatment.

There had been a little doctor, once head of a great European medical college, who had done outstanding research work on the affliction. However, he had been discharged without notice; his blood was tainted with that of an accursed race. Nobody knew where he was staying. But the Dictator was insistent; he was mortal enough to fear death. The little doctor must be found.

The Secret Police rounded him up. He was scrubbing certain filthy streets under the jeering gaze of uniformed petty officials. He came quietly away, his eyes mild and unresentful.

Unflinchingly he stood before the stricken Dictator. "I remember you well," he said musingly. "I operated on you long ago. Before— before ..." he broke off with a sigh.

The Dictator ignored him completely and nodded to a resplendent figure in dress uniform. "Come, swine," snarled the attendant. "The Leader has honored you and your unspeakable race by ordering you to examine him and prescribe treatment. It may be that our gracious Chief will excuse you from street-sweeping if you prove helpful and discreet."

Silently the little doctor made his preparations and began the examination. After a final scrutiny of the x-ray plates taken of the patient's thoracic cavity, he addressed himself to the Dictator.

"I concur in the diagnosis of your surgeons," he said quietly. "But I believe that your only good chance for recovery lies in the new treatment by artificial fever induced by short-wave radio. I found it highly effective in my research investigations."

The attending surgeons glanced at each other reprovingly. Why had not that idea occurred to them? The Dictator nodded meaningly toward the little doctor, and a guard seized his arm.

"Well, swine," snapped the official. "Would you insult the Leader further with your unclean presence? Come; we will take you where no one will ever hear you boast that our glorious Chief sent for you."

They led him out. He was never seen again.

As soon as possible the fever machine was brought from an experimental hospital. The young technician, awed by the eminence of his patient, was manifestly nervous, but he exhibited complete faith in his equipment. Carefully he removed the Dictator's massive rings, explaining that the short waves heated metal to an unbearable temperature very rapidly.

Under the suspicious eyes of the ever-present guards, the Dictator was comfortably settled beside the complex machine. After a final examination, the technician switched on the current. The soothing hum of the apparatus filled the quiet chamber.

Abruptly the Dictator half arose, a cry of pain and terror on his lips. Horrified, the technician snapped the switch. Too late; the Dictator emitted a single gasp and died.

The little doctor, now dead, and in an unmarked grave, had well remembered the operation upon the Dictator during which he had inserted a platinum plate in the young patient's skull. A plate, which heated white-hot by the impinging short-waves, had seared consciousness and life from the diseased brain.

# When the Sleeper Wakes

The bartender of the cantina stared disapprovingly at the diminutive form snoring vigorously in a rickety chair. "In about two minutes," he rumbled, "I'm gonna throw that little drifter out. Been here nigh onto two hours and ain't even bought a shot!" He advanced meaningly toward the unconscious culprit.

Young Bob Trevis who sat moodily at a nearby table hailed him. "Go on, Soapy," he called good-naturedly. "Let the old guy sleep; he ain't doing no harm. Looks like he come a long way, too."

Soapy grunted and nodded grudging assent. "Okay if you say so, Bob, but I ain't running no flophouse."

The swinging doors flew open and a bowlegged little cowpuncher hurried over to Bob's table. "Better light outta here," he cautioned Trevis in low tones. "Blackie Carew and two of his gun-slicks are heading here to make trouble. He's been talking up about how you've had your warning to keep away from Betty Rutherford. C'mon, Bob, scoot outta here quick!"

Trevis shook his head, his face white but resolute. "I'm sick of ducking Blackie and his hired killers," he snapped. "Might just as well get plugged as have folks calling you yellow."

"Nobody's calling you that, Bob. Why, any one of the three of 'em could plug you before you cleared leather—even Blackie himself.

Listen, if you'll just clear outta town for a couple of weeks, maybe we can sorta organize and run 'em out."

"I'm staying, I tell you," grated Trevis, loosening his gun in its holster. "Maybe I can down one of 'em after I stop lead—one shot's all I'll need!"

His friend shook his head despairingly. "Ace Wilks and Slick Harris are tagging along with Blackie. Either one of 'em can outdraw anybody in these parts. Heard tell Ace beat Kid Canty over at Cottonwood yesterday. Why, this woozy little drifter here would have a better chance than you!"

As if in response to the bitter comment the sleeper opened one eye to disclose a patch of filmy blue, and closed it again to the accompaniment of a rasping gurgle.

A sudden hush fell over the crowd as Blackie Carew stepped catfootedly into the room. His flaring yellow eyes surveyed the crowd challengingly. Then he spied Bob Trevis and advanced stiff-leggedly toward his table.

"So the poor little child was finally let outta the nursery," he began sneeringly. "You're a hard man to find, Trevis. Person might think you was afraid to be found in the open. Kinda reminds me of a certain yellow-backed critter what don't smell too good. Can't see what the ladies like about your baby face!"

Travis' eyes blazed, and he rose deliberately from his chair. "I know what's eating you, Blackie. You're a mangy skunk what ain't got guts enough to be a sport."

Carew laughed gloatingly. "Don't tell me you're gonna make a play for that pretty ornament at your hip, Trevis. It takes more nerve than you've got to make a play for anything but women."

Bob flushed and his drawing arm tensed for the hopeless attempt.

A gentle, weary voice broke the action-impending silence. "You boys has plumb ruined a perfectly good snooze," the drifter yawned. "Now you," he continued, stretching his arms and then pointing at Blackie, "you're all het up and full of pizen, as you might say. Nothing like a good sleep to take that outta a man. A real good sleep can—"

Blackie broke in with a snarl. "What the hell do you want, you old fool?" he rasped. "You aiming to mix in this fracas?"

The old man smiled benignly. "Folks back home calls me 'Sleepy'," he admitted cheerfully. "I believe sleep is the great restorer. Knits up the sleeve of care, like Bill Shakespeare says, and—"

He broke off as Carew took a menacing step forward.

"Now listen, you old goat, one more yap outta you, and I'll take and heave you in the watering trough!"

The little man looked bewildered, and his mild blue eyes became watery. "I was just trying to initiate you into the benefits of peaceful sleep. A man full of fury like you needs a long rest to smooth his ruffles kinda."

With an incoherent exclamation Blackie turned his back upon the puzzled Trevis and strode purposefully toward his blinking little victim. Abruptly he stopped and went tense. The drifter stood alert and menacing; the mild blue of his eyes was filmed with ice, and his right hand hung casually free.

Carew laughed hollowly. "Put away that shooting iron, you old bum, before I plug you!" he snapped.

The little drifter swayed slightly and he ran his drawing fingers absently through his thin yellow hair. "Make your play, fella!" he sighed gently.

Like lightning Carew's trained fingers leaped for the smooth butt of his gun. Two shots spanked out and a double puncture appeared as if by magic in Blackie's chest. A look of unbelief swept the rage from his face as he tottered to the floor, his gun barely clear.

Nobody in the awed crowd had seen the drifter's hand move, but a tiny swirl of blue smoke oozed gently from his holster to hang in the air.

"I don't like noisy people who don't let me sleep," he said wearily. "Guess I might as well finish my snooze where I left off 'till the sheriff comes." And without a word to the amazed Bob Trevis, he slumped down in the old chair and closed his eyes.

"Gawd!" muttered one oldster. "Did you see the way he flashed that iron? And look at the holes—a poker chip would cover 'em."

A sudden silence fell upon the buzzing crowd; two sinister figures had burst into the cantina. At the sight of the body upon the floor, Ace Wilks stepped forward. "Hell's fire," he breathed. "It's Blackie!" He turned to a puncher. "Who plugged him?" he demanded. Without a word the man pointed to the sleeping drifter. Bob Trevis watched apprehensively. The two men were Ace Wilks and Slick Harris—plenty mean and plenty fast. Ace approached the sleeper menacingly. "Wake up you son of a bitch!" he roared.

The little man opened an eye and rose lazily to his feet. "Can't a man get no sleep around here?" he protested in a gentle, plaintive voice. "You folks don't seem to realize the value of sleep! Now you take Blackie there; I had to give him a permanent sleep before he'd behave."

The heavy maxillaries in Ace's jaw corded, and his face blackened. "You plugged Blackie, you piece of dirt! And I'm gonna fill you full of lead!"

The mild blue eyes blinked. "Now let's not have no more shooting," the drifter pled. "I can't sleep so well after killing some poor devil. Even Blackie here spoiled my rest now; I gotta uneasy conscience."

"Let's take him," snapped Ace to Slick, while Trevis clutched desperately for his six-gun in a vain effort to help his frail preserver.

Ace was fast, but he didn't have a chance; the little man was a gun artist of the first water. A mere quiver of his arm and the old gun belched two deadly shots. Ace died on his feet, a blue-rimmed hole just above the bridge of his nose. Slick's gun boomed into the floor as a heavy slug tore into his chest. Bob's gun hadn't even cleared leather before it was all over.

In the dead silence that ensued, the little fellow oozed toward the doors, his shoulders hunched wearily. "Going somewhere where I can sleep in peace!" he announced disgustedly, and a moment later the clatter of hoofs marked his departure.

" 'Sleepy'," muttered the dazed Trevis as he wiped cold perspiration from his forehead. "Lord, I'd sure admire to see him wide awake sometime!"

# A Quick Death

It had to be done, and a bullet was best. Quick, and therefore painless. Not too messy either. Now for the right spot. Just in front of the ear? The temple? Or the muzzle against the roof of the mouth? No, not the mouth. Something undignified about that. Face all screwed up as if he were trying to swallow the weapon. The right temple just under the patch of grey. Death would be instantaneous. As a biologist he knew that. The steel-jacketed .45 slug would whip through his skull and brain without even being deformed by its passage.

There—the cool muzzle against the skin. He felt quite calm; his mind was clear and keenly alert. Well, no use waiting. One pull on the trigger, a momentary shock too short lived to exist as pain—then nothing. He had no curiosity as to any hereafter. A materialist to the core, he had long since discarded as untenable all religious speculations touching on death and its possible aftermaths.

His finger tightened on the trigger, taking up the slack gently as he'd learned in the army. All the slack gone—now just a trifle more … what was that rasp of metal on metal? He visualized clearly the familiar structure of the service pistol. The disconnector grating free of the hammer, that was it. But why so loud? The gun hadn't been that neglected. Now a swish—the whistling of heavy metal through the air. That was the hammer describing its irreversible arc toward the waiting firing pin. It struck with a sharp smack, and the pin slid smoothly forward with a mere whisper of sound. Its rounded tip crunched deliberately into the primer of the bullet. A slow hissing followed; the fulminate, jarred into reaction, was hurling its tongue of flame among the cylindrical grains of powder.

He heard the flaming blast hissing through and about the unwilling grains. A long pause. Then one bit of powder took fire with a reluctant sigh to be followed by others, all tossing the flame on with the grave deliberation of old men playing catch.

It was all so incredibly slow. Perhaps he'd better try a different way. He attempted to drop his arm, but it didn't want to move. He willed fiercely, and felt a single tiny muscle fiber knot itself with a mocking lack of haste …

His attention returned to the curious antics of the bullet. It was creaking loudly as the brass cartridge case strained hopelessly against the giant pressure of the super-hot, expanding gases. Unable to resist the rapidly mounting force, the jacketed lead slug slid smoothly from the case, confining its protest to the ghost of a squeak, and brought up with a heavy crunch against the initial grooving of the barrel.

There it paused for a heartbeat as if determined to concede nothing further to the riotous inferno of gas raging for an exit behind it. Then, screeching in a loud monotone that protested the lack of lubrication in the neglected bore, it began its one-way trip down the barrel.

It grated roughly at one point in its journey … that spot of rust he'd planned to remove. Ah! The warm tip of the bullet had at last emerged from the muzzle to press heavily against his damp skin. There was a faint ripping sound as it tore through the skin to meet the hard bone with a solid thump.

Little pattering sounds. The rushing gas carrying fragments of powder, burnt and unburnt, against his forehead. The bullet was crunching relentlessly through the bone, turning slowly and gnawing away like a mouse.

There, it was through! Strong and elastic, the outer membrane of the brain stretched unbearably before snapping to the irresistible thrust of the metal, and the bullet spun easily into the soft tissue of the brain itself. With rain-like patterings and the slow, sobbing ooze of serous fluid, the hot mass of lead and copper moved effortlessly through the tender organ.

A heavy numbness spread over him with the gradual warmth of slow immersion in a hot tub. The bullet rapped peremptorily against the bone that barred its exit, and in the blackness that swirled over him, he heard it resume its grinding progress …

The .45 caliber bullet, hurled by the white-hot gases of the powder, whipped through his skull in one eighteen-hundredth of a second, destroying the brain and conscious existence of the Suicide before his madly racing heart beat once.

The coroner stooped, examined the body with impersonal eyes, and yawned. It was late; suicides always choose the gloomiest hours anyway. He rose and reached for his bag.

"Died instantly," he said with professional assurance.

# No Survivors

When Henry Milton spoke to his neighbors—for he had no friends—about the end of the world being imminent, they didn't even laugh at him. They merely nodded almost imperceptibly in agreement and hurried on, leaving Milton to dilate on his discovery to the unheeding air.

But Milton seemed not to care greatly whether the villagers believed him or not. He knew. Not for nothing had he been for years an ardent student of astronomy, as his numerous contributions to the astronomical journals testified. With his small but effective refracting telescope, he had, but a few years before, discovered a new asteroid. His achievements along astronomical lines had been greatly aided by the fact that atmospheric conditions about his little observatory in the Maine woods were conducive to stellar observation. Although Milton, at least, credited his accomplishments to his own ability.

It had been a fortunate thing indeed that his aunt had left him such a tidy sum in government bonds when she died; but, nevertheless, it was no more than he deserved. Any qualms he may have entertained about receiving the money were quickly dispelled when he remembered that he had, after all, named the asteroid after her!

But now, his greatest find was given no credence. Scientists refused to believe that the dark star Milton had glimpsed with the aid of an instrument of his own invention was hurtling with unthinkable velocity toward our sun and its attendant planets.

Milton fumed, swore, and wrote dozens of scathing letters, but to no avail. The scientific world laughed heartily at first and then merely regarded him as a nuisance. So Henry Milton ceased his efforts to convince a skeptical people, and commenced the construction of what a village wag named immediately 'Milton's Folly'.

Set firmly upon the top of a small granite formation, it was an immensely strong, dome-like structure of steel alloy and super-concrete. The carefully padded and spring-supported interior contained all that was needed to sustain life over a long period of time, from tins of concentrated nourishment to the great oxygen tanks that lined the windowless walls. If the shock were not too great, there might be one survivor—and Milton meant to be that one.

Despite the gibes of the townspeople, Milton held his peace and tried vainly to catch another glimpse of the dark star, the direction and speed of which he wished to verify.

At length came the inevitable day when the giant star, black and dead though it was, caught the eye of many an astronomer. The Mount Wilson Observatory, with its mighty two-hundred-inch reflector, had the dubious honor of being the first to verify the statements of Henry Milton. Shortly after, word flashed from the Greenwich Observatory. They too found it bulking large and menacing against the crosshairs; and as soon as radio and telegraph could transmit the startling news, every telescope in the civilized world was sweeping the heavens.

The first newspaper to break the story carried the following headline on its front page:

EARTH MAY BE DOOMED!
DEAD WORLD SWEEPING TOWARD SOLAR SYSTEM!

Underneath was told in minute detail, with a sprinkling of mathematical formulae, how the black star, invisible hitherto because of its non-reflecting surface, with a mass billions of times greater than the earth's, would sweep the moon like a speck from the sky and strip the racked earth of nine-tenths of its atmosphere.

And twenty-four hours later, as astronomer after astronomer admitted the accuracy of Milton's calculations, the world went entirely mad, with milling mobs fighting in the streets for the privilege of looting and burning.

Henry Milton, meanwhile, had been sleeping in a small cabin near his refuge—sleeping as it were with one eye open, for though the stolid villagers were slow to become panicky, they were nevertheless showing a reawakened interest in Milton's Folly. This Milton had foreseen, and among his readily accessible supplies was a deadly automatic rifle.

One night, Milton awakened suddenly, and perceiving that the sky was red, wasted little time in getting into his clothes and hurrying over to unlock his metal vault. Leaving the massive door ajar, he stood in the clear and gazed with morbid fascination at the brilliant tints that flashed in rapid succession across the crimson sky. Little he knew of the panic that reigned in the great cities of the world, where shrieking mobs milled like ants in the quivering streets.

He could see in the distance the flaming tops of great pines. The forest was afire. Several small animals scurried by him almost unnoticed. Abruptly his ears caught the sound of voices. Approaching him from the direction of the village was a large crowd. The crisis Milton had predicted was upon him and he was prepared. Leisurely he entered the vault, noticing subconsciously as he did so, a strange, musty odor. Moments later he emerged clutching the rifle in steady fingers.

As the clamoring mob swept nearer, Milton raised the gun to his shoulder. Beads of perspiration stood out on his forehead and he closed his eyes in anguish.

"God forgive me," he muttered between clenched teeth. Then his mouth tightened into a thin hard line and his finger pressed the trigger. Men, women, and children crumpled into little rag-like bundles under the deadly fire, and the survivors broke and fled.

With his face grey and old, Henry Milton entered his steel chamber, and tossing the hot gun into a corner, threw his full weight against the door and swung the ponderous time-locks to.

Behind him, there emerged from between two packing cases a lithe, tawny form. Terrified by the forest fire, a giant cougar had crept through the half-opened door into Milton's Folly.

Milton turned about with a sigh of relief. His eyes met the flaring yellow ones of the pain-maddened beast. For a heartbeat he stood as one paralyzed, seeming to gaze dispassionately at the cougar's seared flanks. Then his glance flicked to the rifle and back to the crouching cat that stood between. Ever so slowly, an ironical smile twisted his lips.

"Well, Kitty," he said quietly, soothingly, as he attempted to hold the beast with his glance, "it's still the survival of the fittest!" Then he lunged desperately for the gun.

And even as the dying earth quivered in the mighty gravitational clutch of the dead star, the great cat met him halfway …

# The Terror of the Mindanao Depths

"Such nonsense I will listen to no longer. This is not science; this is charlatanism!" And the worthy and weighty Doctor Hans Jakob, his whole body quivering with indignation, his face not unlike an impressionist's sunset, made a bull-like exit which almost disrupted three seats and four of my toes.

At the unceremonious and noisy departure of the famous Berlin psychiatrist, the speaker paused for a moment, his deep-set eyes under their shaggy black brows surveying the audience with an expression midway between amusement and contempt. As he stood there, a tall, commanding figure, his rugged features showed nothing of the disappointment and chagrin the derisive reception of his speech should have aroused.

I was deeply puzzled at such a lack of concern upon the part of McAllister since, after all, he was explaining the theory and construction of his own amazing mechanism—the Thought-Compass. It was standing beside him—a wonderfully conceived and brilliantly constructed device, whose needle, carved from a single rare osmium crystal, was poised delicately among five powerful magnetic fields operating in a near-perfect vacuum.

That such a device could actually detect thought-energy was difficult enough for a hard-bitten crew of research men to swallow, but when McAllister actually claimed for the compass the ability to distinguish good thoughts from bad, a swelling murmur of derision broke from the scientific gathering.

Two rows ahead of me the sharp-tongued Royal Naylor Dwight, the most positive objective psychologist who ever tormented his misguided colleagues for incautious references to such intangibles as "mind" and "moral force," leaped to his feet to fling a challenge in the teeth of the calm-faced Franklin McAllister.

Dwight was a clever, much-feared debater. He had once squelched a famous mystic with the acid—and entirely sophistical—remark that the only thing certain to be accurately reflected in a crystal was the face of some gullible jackass peering into it. Perhaps Dwight might have been less skeptical had he been capable of following the ultra-complex radiation mathematics of Dr. McAllister. After all, this was the same McAllister who crashed the "Fundamenta Mathematica" with a forty-page paper on "The Existence and Non-Existence of Isoenergetic Periodic Perturbations of the Disturbed Circular Motions in the Unrestricted Problems of N Bodies in Hyperspace." But Dwight's mathematical background included little beyond educational statistics, and he was used to speaking his piece, especially if the audience were large enough. And McAllister gave him the floor with just such a tight little smile as an old pussycat wears when the mouse's whiskers start to edge out of the hole.

Dwight was not slow to respond. "Dr. McAllister," he began in his crisp, incisive voice, "I should like to see you focus this—this mental gumshoe of yours on a certain European statesman who keeps his thoughts too much to himself."

A ripple of laughter came from the seats at this sally, for Europe was in a sad muddle only five years after the eighth world war to end all wars.

Dwight's voice grew sharper. "I have nothing but respect for your attainments in the field of experimental psychology, but when you attempt to convince such an audience as this,"—here a note of complacency crept into his voice—"made up of experienced research men, that there are any absolute standards of good or evil, all the fancy mathematical analysis in the world is inadequate to substantiate such balderdash. You have said that your present Thought-Compass is too crude to react to the thoughts of less than 5,000 people concentrating in unison. I wonder if the fact that this hall seats exactly 4,500 had anything to do with the limit of sensitivity." And Dwight seated himself amid a gale of laughter in which I joined, despite myself.

At that moment young Harvey Albert slipped into Jakob's empty seat. "Why the devil don't that bunch of old fogeys stop making fools of themselves?" he growled. "His mathematical development was the sweetest thing I've seen since Rufus Lundheimer proved Fermat's Last Theorem in the July 'Transactions.' "

"You're right," I agreed gloomily. "I minored in psychology under McAllister, and a more canny, cautious worker I've never met. He's worth fifty like Dwight."

"But that crack of his about a thought-source in the Mindanao Deep—" Albert began in a puzzled tone, only to break off as McAllister resumed his speech.

"We may not classify thoughts *absolutely* as 'good' or 'evil'," McAllister said, "but the Thought-Compass has indicated a classification as significant as any absolute divisions might be. We all know that although it might be good for M to kill D,"—here he glanced significantly at Dwight and the audience roared its delight at the thrust—"it is not good for D to be killed by M. But what is it that may be used to distinguish one thought from another? The answer is not difficult.

"Consider the thought 'Carthage must be destroyed.' Here we have a suggestion conducive to positive action. We may call such a suggestion evil. A neutral thought would be 'Let us calmly and fairly examine our relations with Carthage,' while a good, or action-negating thought may be characterized by 'Carthage is certainly no menace to us; let's forget about her.' This is the manner in which the Thought-Compass identifies thought-energy—purely artificial, often overlapping, but at least a start in the right direction. Now I have told you—much to your amusement—that this model, too insensitive to react to the concentrated thinking of less than 5,000 people has definitely located a thought-source of inestimable power in the 34,000 foot Mindanao Deep off the Philippines. Certain check-tests of mine—such as reprojection of the suggestions to small animals—have convinced me that the thought-energy emanating from this hole in the sea-bottom is of inconceivable power and malignancy. Gentlemen, you may well account me mad, but I believe that whoever or whatever is the origin of this mental radiation is more than a little responsible for many of the woes of mankind—and for war in particular."

The audience sat in a stunned silence after McAllister's astounding statement, and his next words made a break in the hush that was almost painful to the hearing.

"I should like to hear from Sir Arthur Mannering on the feasibility of descending 34,000 feet into the Mindanao Deep," was McAllister's cool request. Albert looked at me with such a ludicrous expression on his face that I chuckled.

Mannering was almost incapable of showing enthusiasm about anything; he was the ice-blooded Englishman personified, but a keen observer readily might have inferred that McAllister's audacious idea was near to his own heart. Briefly he discussed a plan that seemed to him quite practicable.

It was based on the work of the twentieth-century scientists Beebe and Piccard, and utilized the latter's ingenious descent mechanism. A hollow metal sphere, lighter when fully loaded than an equal volume of water, could be sunk to any depth by means of iron balls held firmly in a cup-like hollow of the base by a powerful electromagnet. Once upon the sea-bottom, the craft could employ some efficient means of propulsion to explore the surrounding regions. At any time the current to the electromagnet could be broken, dropping the iron balls and allowing the sphere to rise rapidly to the surface.

"There are difficult problems of design," Mannering concluded in his impersonal, almost bored tones, "but we have alloys today which can take almost any amount of punishment, and given the funds I am convinced a successful descent could be made." And to the great astonishment of all that knew him the Englishman added enthusiastically: "By Jove, I'd like to design such a craft!"

Once again McAllister's voice cut into the rising murmur. "Gentlemen, I intend to make the descent very soon, and I shall have the pleasure of shattering your skepticism then. Therefore I shall make no further efforts in that direction today." And with a slight bow he strode briskly from the stage, leaving the audience uncertain whether to laugh or applaud.

Immediately I fought my way through the crowd and headed backstage to offer my encouragement and support to one of the few truly great men I had ever known. But although I got there quickly, two men were there before me. One of them, as might have been suspected, was Sir Arthur Mannering. The other I recognized as Lars P. Gunnarson, an engineering genius who had been known to construct precision equipment from mere junk. It was rumored that he could run a diesel engine on condensed milk, and such was the esteem in which this plump, little man was held that many engineers actually believed it. At any rate, in the event of engine trouble—were the engine anything from a toy spring-motor to a ten-ton steam-generator setup—Gunnarson was worth the whole roster of any engineering society. Such was the man who was talking earnestly to McAllister as I entered the room.

At the sight of me McAllister smiled a welcome. "I thought you'd be here, Lambert," he said. "I read that last paper of yours in 'Science'—the one that reclassified the Ctenophora. I don't know a damned thing about it myself, but it must have been hot stuff, because Doc Jordan was running around in circles wishing he'd signed you up before the Research Foundation grabbed you." Naturally I blushed, what with Gunnarson smiling up at me benignly like a good elf, and told them how much of the hard work had been done by my graduate assistants.

But McAllister just grinned skeptically and changed the subject. "Sir Arthur is willing to design the ship," McAllister told me, as his fingers toyed with his watch-chain. "And Gunnarson is itching to get to work on a new fangled power plant. Lambert, I'd like to have you along for deep-sea fauna and photography—we may need photographic evidence to convince those skeptics out there."

"B-but," I stammered, "you'll need money to build such a ship; in fact, you'll need a small fortune."

McAllister smiled. "Never mind about the money," he reassured me. "I spoke to someone before delivering the address. He doesn't know much about mathematics, but he knows me, and he's as keen for unusual scientific ventures as a kid is for Wild West movies. Not to mention the fact that he has about four thousand dollars for every Smith in the New York Telephone Directory."

"Who in the Devil—?" I began, when somebody rapped vigorously on the door. I turned to open it, admitting a stoop-shouldered old man who sidled in after the manner of a nervous hermit crab. Of course, I recognized him immediately as almost anybody would. Ezra Hannibal Prouty was the only multimillionaire actively engaged in research work; he patented about fifty inventions a year and made money so darned fast he couldn't even give it away.

"Who's the young whippersnapper?" he snorted with a nod in my direction. "I thought I was to be kept anonymous."

"This is Glenn Lambert," McAllister introduced me. "He knows more about the private life of every creature that floats, swims, or sinks in salt water than any other zoologist in the world. I'm counting him in on our little party, so your confidence has been respected."

"Looks husky enough," grunted Prouty, squinting at me with a pair of amazingly sharp eyes. "Football, I reckon."

"Right the first time," said McAllister. "All American, too."

"We could get to business, yes?" queried Gunnarson, as if anxious to start designing equipment immediately. Mannering nodded approval, with equal impatience.

"Business is over," growled Prouty. "Frank here talked me out of a fortune before he spoke to them overeducated monkeys out there. Didn't you notice how cocky he was?" He pawed at his vest-pocket, shifted to the coat, muttered imprecations, and finally fished a limp paper from a hip pocket. This he handed to McAllister with a satisfied snort. "And don't forget to keep me informed, young fellow," he admonished the middle-aged psychologist, "or I'll hire somebody to build a bigger one and go down myself. I'm almost ready to do it, by

Heaven!" Whereupon he sidled out, leaving us all gaping at a check for $300,000 on the biggest bank in the country.

With such a sum credited to McAllister's account, preparations proceeded rapidly. Sir Mannering designed a graceful, spherical shell large enough to hold three men comfortably, and strong enough to withstand any pressure not in excess of 20,000 pounds per square inch. Since the pressure at 34,000 feet could not be greater than 15,000 pounds per square inch, there was an adequate margin of safety. The four ports were a double thickness of transparent concillium, ground and fitted to form huge achromatic lenses in the practically indestructible tungsten-iridium hull. With the aid of a large Shumaki-Clarke cold light generator clear vision was possible through a full hundred yards of unclouded water. The caterpillar treads, broad enough to support the great mass of the sphere even on semi-liquid mud, were powered by independent twin Miracle engines, those wonderful power plants that delivered hundreds of horsepower per ounce of nitrolene fuel.

In the most ticklish matter of all, the packing where the drive shafts issued from the hull into six miles of crushing mass, Lars Gunnarson had displayed his full genius. The sleek argon-indium rods that transmitted the power of the engine to the mighty treads were surrounded at the hull by eight different packing substances, including an inner core of graphite dust suspended in molten wax. The latter was kept liquid by iron particles under the influence of an induced current.

To effect a safe landing on the floor of Mindanao, Gunnarson had built extensible diving planes, which together with lightened ballast would suffice to deposit the craft with almost no shock.

And just in case an opportunity arose to destroy the entity we sought, the grim mouths of four stubby torpedo tubes commanded a 360-degree field about the sphere. Such was the mechanical marvel we gathered to christen and test one morning early in April.

"How does she look to you, Glenn?" McAllister asked me, as we leaned over the rail of Ezra Prouty's seagoing yacht to gaze at our sphere, which was firmly lashed alongside.

"With that round, jointed hull of hers," I answered offhand, "she looks like an overgrown diatom."

"She does, at that," laughed McAllister. And before I knew it, he and Gunnarson had cracked a bottle of wine over the metal hull of the "Diatom."

As for the testing, there seemed to be only one practical and effective way of going about it, and that was plenty risky. We had to drop her fully loaded to the bottom of Mindanao Deep, where a trip-lever would release the ballast and allow her to rise—if she hadn't shipped a few tons of water in the meantime. Gunnarson rigged up a pressure-operated unit to lighten her when she was a few hundred feet from the bottom, but for over 33,000 feet the Diatom was to drop as fast as she could go. In a vacuum the fall would have taken her only 45 seconds, but in water—well, the darn thing was down over half an hour, and McAllister's face had gone grey as he pictured the $250,000 ball buried in the mud with its hull stove in by the inconceivable weight of the liquid about it.

Then there was a whoosh and a roar as the Diatom, glittering like an immense jewel because of the seawater pouring over her jointed hull, leaped high in the air to fall back with a mighty splash. Well, she was dry as a bone inside, all right, but that last kangaroo act of hers gave Gunnarson a few things to think about, and he made us hold off until he'd made arrangements for strapping us firmly in our seats.

At last the annoying final details were taken care of, and we were ready to slip our cable and sink beneath the surface in the wildest and most fantastic quest that three men had ever undertaken.

Just before the hatch was dogged down—as if it needed any fastening with six miles of salt water squatting on it—McAllister handed Gunnarson and me each an odd-looking helmet of some light alloy with a little Miller Battery and control dial over the left ear. There was also a small krypton bulb on top of the contraption.

"Put them on," McAllister advised us with a slightly grim smile. "I think you'll need them before long." I was about to demand an explanation, but McAllister clapped a helmet over his own bushy head, waved a final goodbye to Ezra Prouty—who was scuttling about the deck of his yacht heckling everybody from the captain to the deckhands—and Gunnarson and I were both hustled into the Diatom before we knew it.

There ensued a few tense moments as Gunnarson closed and dogged down the port and McAllister hesitated before giving the order that would drop us 34,000 feet into unknown waters—waters that might conceal some grim and terrible secret. Then he sighed; a little smile of satisfaction touched his mobile lips, and at his curt nod Gunnarson threw the cable release.

Almost regretfully, as if reluctant to quit the sunny blue surface, the Diatom plunged into the quiet water. Swiftly the greenish tint shifted to grey, and finally to the inkiest black as the great metal ball fell with a sickening acceleration that not even the tremendous resistance of the water could—at least at first—noticeably allay.

Many fish fled from us in terror, only to dive alongside as if fascinated by the piercing beam of our searchlight. In particular the dainty demoiselles could not resist its hypnotic glow and crossed and re-crossed it in a rainbow display that had my two companions enthralled. It was old stuff to me; I'd spent half my life in glass-bottomed boats and diving rigs studying tropical fish, but as we dropped breathtakingly lower into the abysmal depths, I too began to strain my eyes along the path of the beam. Now we were past the Beebe level; no man had ever been lower—alive. The resistance of the water held our velocity almost constant, and my companions had lost interest in mere fish. McAllister crouched over the brain of the ship—the sensitive and wonderfully mounted Thought-Compass whose needle pointed almost straight down on its universal magnetic pivot. Gunnarson kept his eyes glued to the depth gauge and fussed with the jewel-like power plant.

At 20,000 feet I glimpsed a monstrous sinuous form dotted with phosphorescent lights like some great liner of the lower depths. My cry of ecstatic wonder made McAllister turn his head, but the stolid Gunnarson paid no attention even in time to see the twenty-foot glowing tail sweep by.

Then about 8,000 feet lower something hurtled through the beam that made my heart miss a beat. McAllister and Gunnarson saw it too, and they looked at me as if to say: "If you saw what we did, for God's sake, what was it?" I couldn't tell them what it was, for certain, but judging from the blurred photograph I examined later it was a sea serpent as long as a good-sized freight train—and about ten times faster.

"You'd better hold tight now," Gunnarson warned us mildly. "We've got less than five hundred feet left to go." Silently McAllister and I braced ourselves for a shock. But we reckoned without the skill of Gunnarson, for under his expert fingers the Diatom, lightened of many of its iron balls, and under the support of the broad diving planes, settled gently on the firm, sandy seabed.

McAllister was all for heading in the direction indicated by the Thought-Compass, but the canny Gunnarson insisted on retrieving as many of the ballast balls as possible first, lest the Diatom should be too light for proper traction.

So McAllister curbed his impatience by taking a distance reading from the Thought-Compass while the Diatom, giant shafts whirling in their wonderful packing, crept about like some great denizen of the deep. Within a few minutes the Diatom's mighty electromagnet had recaptured most of the released iron balls.

Abruptly the psychologist whirled from the Thought-Compass after timing the oscillations of a tiny platinum pendulum. "Fourteen seconds!" he snapped, obviously surprised. "We're practically on top of the damned thing."

I leaped to the nearest port and stared out across the seabed. The powerful achromatic lenses brought everything within range of the beam into clear, glowing focus, but all I could see was sand blending into rocky soil at the limit of my vision.

Then I heard a choked cry, and turned about as a red, murderous rage swept over me. I realized that I hated McAllister and Gunnarson as no two men had ever been hated before. And this grotesque, silly craft of ours; it would be sweet to wreck its wonderful mechanisms and leave it silent and dead on the floor of Mindanao. As I half arose to clutch at McAllister his hand brushed my head with a single lightning-like movement, and all my rage left me to be replaced by horror. For Gunnarson, his face set in a demoniac grin, was lurching toward the controls, a heavy wrench in his fist poised for a mighty stroke, and the little krypton bulb in his helmet winking a sickly green.

Like a tiger I sprang at him, and so great was his mad strength, that although I outweighed him by many pounds, I needed all my football-trained strength to overcome him.

"Hold him, Glenn," McAllister snapped in a cool, unshaken voice, and reaching over my shoulder he snapped the dial on Gunnarson's helmet. The little man heaved desperately for a moment and then relaxed as a sheepish smile touched his lips.

"I've been acting very silly, don't you think?" he inquired mildly.

McAllister smiled his relief. "Let him go, Glenn; he'll be all right now, but lord, that was too close for comfort there for a while."

"What—what in the devil is it all about?" I stammered. "I felt like murder myself for a minute."

"I have no time now to explain," gritted the psychologist. "That thing—whatever it is—was expecting us and did its damnedest to make us destroy ourselves. And like a prize fool I helped it by forgetting to put on the current in your thought-shields. But let's get busy; start her up, Gunnarson."

Once more the broad caterpillar treads bit into the firm sand, and the newly weighted Diatom crawled inexorably forward under the thrust of its mighty twin engines. We turned far to the left once to avoid a black pit in the sand—an awful well that looked bottomless. Was this more of the entity's doing?

As our craft swung back into line with the violently quivering needle of the Thought-Compass, McAllister uttered a sharp exclamation which Gunnarson and I echoed as the glaring beam revealed a truly astounding sight.

Half imbedded in the iron-hard sand and silt of untold centuries, a great crystalline cylinder loomed up before us. Through its transparent sides we glimpsed mighty machines of silvery metals—machines whose myriad complex connections would have baffled the best technicians on earth. But it was the thing in the cylinder that drained the blood from our faces and made even the phlegmatic Gunnarson draw back in horror.

As I look back to that eventful day, I find it easy to liken the monster to an enormous brain, but that tendency may be traced directly to the inconceivable mental power we knew it possessed—and still possesses, I fear. Actually, it was more like a huge broken egg splattered on the floor of the cylinder—a broken egg whose sickly green yolk pulsed and throbbed with malignant force; an egg with a huge purple eye in the center.

The bravest act of my life was to seize the infrared telescopic camera and sight it at the horror. I have the print before me now—faked, they said when I was foolish enough to offer it in evidence. It shows the tiny, cut off compartment in the cylinder that broke McAllister's heart.

But not even the sight of the nightmarish thing could weaken the psychologist's grim determination. Calling out curt directions to the pale Gunnarson he sprang to the forward torpedo tubes, waiting tight-lipped as the Diatom rolled inexorably closer to the cylinder and its raging occupant.

When we had reached a point beyond which the explosion of the torpedoes might seriously endanger our sphere, McAllister aligned the frowning muzzles and released two of the deadly Whitehead-Currier missiles.

One of them reached its mark, but the other, before our incredulous gaze was intercepted by a dully phosphorescent, hurtling form as some giant of the deep took the terrific force of the detonating nitrolene on its scaly side.

As the creature disappeared in a blast of intolerable flame, and the Diatom quivered violently to the shock of the explosion, the other torpedo struck fairly against the side of the cylinder. The junction of the two explosive waves flung the weighty mass of our sphere back like a pebble, to pause on its stern for a single endless moment before dropping back to its treads.

It took only a few moments for the heavy sand stirred up by the explosions to settle, and to our great delight an ominous-looking crack marred the pristine surface of the cylinder. But no water had entered it as yet, and McAllister hastily realigned the grim tubes for the final blasts. Then it happened with stunning rapidity; a thing unbelievable.

Although the monstrosity in the crystal tube—shot hence from some other world perhaps eons before—could not help itself, the mighty mental power it wielded brought a host of terrible allies to its aid.

Before McAllister could fire the next two torpedoes, the water was veritably alive with the fantastic creatures of the Mindanao depths. A purple stingray as large as an omnibus splattered a port with yellow venom as its barbed appendage whipped the lens like a giant flail. Smaller fish hurled themselves in streams against the ports and torpedo tubes, completely blocking McAllister's aim even if he had dared to risk a premature explosion. And approaching slowly and inexorably as fate itself, its hundred foot jet-black arms reaching out like clutching fingers as it clashed a horny beak the size of a man, came a nightmare of the sea-floor—a colossal octopus such as no man had ever seen before. Surely this horror of the deep was no cousin to the little three-foot octopus I had once captured in southern waters.

Desperately Gunnarson whipped the Diatom from right to left in an effort to obtain a clear shot for the hard-eyed McAllister, while I, hanging on grimly, worked my camera like a demon.

Then an arm of immense power coiled about the sphere to be followed soon after by others. Suckers large as platters gripped the surface, and the gigantic mass of the metal sphere was shaken like a doll in the hands of a child.

Grimly we clung to our holds, and despite the terrific lurching of the craft, Gunnarson worked quickly over the powerful dynamos, his stubby fingers performing mechanical and electrical magic. Not even the horror of our position could quell the admiration within me as I saw that bald little man creating circuits and amplifying units with a speed and precision that were uncanny. His end attained, he clung tightly to a stanchion as the monstrous octopus literally lifted the heavy Diatom from the ocean bed. Risking a broken neck, Gunnarson then leaped for a switch and threw it, releasing the full amperage of the generators into the outer hull. No protoplasm could take such a current; the eight-armed horror dropped the sphere six feet to the sand and thrashed about in agony. But even then the creature thwarted us, for the water grew black with the great gouts of ink it excreted—ink that cut off the cold light beam as effectively as a solid wall.

There we sat waiting for the water to clear, wondering what devilment the alien entity in the cylinder would be up to in the meantime.

"That cylinder must be made of the toughest stuff anybody ever saw," groaned McAllister. "Why, I've seen one of these torpedoes shatter a 12-inch beryllium-chrome plate like cheese—not to mention God knows how many yards of wood and concrete backing."

"We've got the damned critter plenty worried," I consoled him. "And after all, the cylinder *is* cracked."

Abruptly Gunnarson stiffened. "We are moving!" he cried hoarsely, and at the same instant the Diatom gave a sudden backward lurch. McAllister sprang to the rear port and exclaimed in dismay. I followed his gaze and saw with horror the tangled web of rope-like material that had been wrapped or spun about the sphere. A single thick strand of the same stuff led off into the murk of the water. Hastily I swung the beam about, and to my dying day I'll never forget the sight that met my gaze.

There are some things that transcend mere human power of description. Surely no sane man would attempt to portray the gibbering thing that pursues him through the eternal duration of a nightmare. Yet since I wish this account to be complete—though I be called mad for it—I shall endeavor to describe that which is truly indescribable.

Picture a spider, the most loathsome, malignant spider your mind can conceive, and imagine that it is enlarged to the size of a two-story bungalow. Think of such a horror covered with clotted, spiny hair that literally writhes and ripples with malignant energy. Such is a weak image of the hideous monster that had spun a net about us and was attempting to drag our sphere off into the uncharted depths of the Mindanao Deep. I turned cold as I thought of that bottomless pit we had passed earlier.

But Gunnarson had boundless faith in the power plant he had built, and didn't hesitate to match its might with that of the eight-legged nightmare. He seized the controls; the mighty twin engines roared into life and the treads bit into the soil with the full inconceivable energy of the atomically decomposing Ferrite solution.

Time after time the gigantic spider dragged the enormous mass of the Diatom back several yards, only to have the racing engines regain the lost ground as the grim-faced Gunnarson opened the throttle wide.

Then McAllister, although he was reluctant to use one of the last two torpedoes, sighted carefully and fired, sending the slender missile streaking through the icy water made murky by the spider's titanic lunges. Squarely and heavily the little torpedo struck the globular, hairy body, and when the silt had settled, he saw that the nitrolene had done its work well. Save for a few scattered bits of flesh the creature was no more.

Once again we were free to turn our attention to the alien being in the cylinder. To our delight the crack had lengthened; water was oozing in, and McAllister gave a cry of triumph. But he exulted too soon, for realizing the fate that awaited it once the sea gained entrance, the monster deliberately tore itself in two. The small portion, containing only a hundredth of the original bulk, crawled rapidly toward the separate little compartment that was undamaged. McAllister was cursing in a low, intense voice, his eyes bright with purpose.

"We've got to stop it; it's getting away," he gritted, and the heavy maxillaries in his jaw corded as he sighted the tube containing our last torpedo. There was a deafening roar and a numbing concussion. The torpedo had exploded prematurely in a tube damaged undoubtedly by our recent tussles. The shock of the explosion numbed us for a moment, and when we glimpsed the cylinder the main compartment was flooded, but the small, detached part of the creature was safe in the little chamber. McAllister looked old and haggard, but his eyes still blazed with unquenched determination.

"Full speed ahead, Gunnarson," he rasped, his voice a tense whisper. "I'm going to ram the cylinder."

But the quick eyes of the engineer had spotted the telltale trickle of water where a seam, weakened by the explosion had failed under the titanic thrust of six miles of liquid. Well he knew how quickly such a leak might prove fatal, and with a crackling Norwegian oath—the first I had ever heard him utter—he sprang to the switch controlling the ballast magnet and almost tore it from its seating. Like a rocket the lightened Diatom leaped toward the surface, while the widening seam spewed forth a pencil of water that pierced Gunnarson's arm like a knife.

Well, we made it, and as soon as we came up into the air McAllister and I ripped open the hatch—not without difficulty for many strands of the spider's web still crossed it—and helped outside the wounded Gunnarson. But the Diatom was lost; as soon as we climbed out she sank beneath our feet and plunged back to the icy floor of the Mindanao Deep. About half an hour later we were picked up floating in the sea by Ezra Prouty's ship.

In the months that followed I saw little of McAllister. The experience had made him an embittered man, but when they told him that Ezra Prouty had succumbed to a heart attack, that news completed his breakdown. He was never the same again and seemed to fade away before our eyes. He died about a year after our undersea encounter.

For twenty-five years after that day we have had peace, but in the last few months the War Spirit has been growing stronger. Some of us know why. Down in Mindanao a little piece of the extraterrestrial is growing too … and increasing in mental power. Somehow it must have escaped from its too confining prison and is wreaking its evil will on a helpless mankind.

Gunnarson and I are old; our lives mean little to us, and for years we have prepared for this day. We have a new Diatom; not as good as the old one—for all our penny pinching we fell far short of the necessary funds—but good enough to destroy us and the alien monster of the Mindanao. Everything is in place; we are leaving today. Farewell to all.

*Note: The foregoing manuscript was found on August 20, floating in a metal container off the Philippines. Its incredible story is verified by a single significant fact. Twenty-three hours after the descent of Lambert and Gunnarson, the Confederated European States made honorable peace with the Union of Asiatic Races and both empires disbanded their armies.*

# Denizens of the Drop

Robert "Buddy" Allen, son of the well-known Professor Allen of Blake University, sprang briskly up the stone steps of his father's unpretentious residence, and pressed the bell button vigorously.

He was a tall, blond, boyish-looking young man, deeply tanned, and as he stood before the door a glint of excitement might have been discerned in his merry brown eyes. He pressed the button again impatiently and as he did so, the door swung noiselessly open. Buddy promptly picked up his valises and stepped in. He turned toward the slightly built old man who had responded to his ring, placed his baggage upon the floor, and held out his hand.

"How are you, John?" he asked, with a warm smile.

The old man regarded him in deep astonishment.

"W-why Robert," he stammered, "I thought you were still in South America upon your hunting trip."

"Well, as you see, I'm not," returned Buddy with a boyish grin. "I'm here. Even hunting in South America gets tiresome sometime. Is the guv'nor in?"

"Professor Allen is in his study, Robert. He'll be delighted to see you again."

"Oh yeah? He'll probably hand me a ticket to Asia this time! But lead ahead." Smiling, the old servant led the way down a dimly lighted hallway and stopped before a massive oak door. He knocked softly.

"Well?" demanded a bull-like voice from within.

"There's someone here to see you, professor," said John, with a wink at the grinning Buddy.

"I can't be bothered now, Keeton. Tell him to come back tomorrow—or next year!" Buddy pushed Keeton gently aside, opened the door and stepped quickly into a large room that was evidently being used as a laboratory, as the walls were fitted with many shelves filled with chemicals and apparatus.

"I beg your pardon, my dear Professor Allen," he said suavely, "but if you can spare me just a moment of your very valuable time, I'm sure that—"

The man who had been seated before a low desk on which was standing a large microscope, looked up in surprise at the sound of Buddy's voice.

"Well I'll be—" he interrupted, "it's Buddy!" He rose to his feet, and as he did so, one could see with half an eye that he was an exception to the generally accepted description of a great scientist.

Professor William T. Allen was at least an inch over six feet. His broad forehead, over two piercing brown eyes, was covered by the strands that had strayed from his great, bushy shock of flaming red hair. It was not hard to see, as he stood there, why he had captained his college's eleven, or why he had led in scholarship upwards of several thousands of other pupils, for four years.

As he shook hands heartily with his son, he said in a tone of inquiry, "I thought you were in So—"

"I know," broke in Buddy, wearily, "I'm supposed to be jaguar chasing, but I've had enough traveling and so called adventure, Dad. They told me a jaguar was a pretty tough customer, but heck, I got pretty close to about five of the darn things and never was in the slightest danger. I even got a couple of great snapshots. They're no more dangerous than house cats!"

"You were probably lucky in your encounters; in fact I'm sure you were. However, I gather that you're ready to quit adventuring and to settle down." He spoke in a tone that held a hint of disappointment, and Buddy looked at him keenly.

"Not at all," he said quickly. "But I don't see where there's any to be found."

"Sit down," said his father calmly, "and perhaps I can enlighten you. Just what do you know about science? Biology, for instance?"

"Practically nothing," stated Buddy, shamelessly.

Professor Allen regarded him in disgust. "Did you ever hear of an animal known as a Paramecium?" he demanded.

"Paramecium. Hmm. Sounds somewhat familiar. Where does the critter hang out? I've seen just about everything else!"

"Never mind. Forget it, at least for the present." His voice became serious. "While you were gone, I made a very important discovery relative to the effect of high frequency sound waves upon matter, which I'll attempt to explain to you. Now, as you probably know—or should—sound is transmitted to our ears by means of waves that are propagated through the air by some vibrating body. These sound waves vary greatly as to the number of vibrations per second. For instance, a body vibrating sixteen times per second produces the lowest sound we can hear, while a body at a rate of forty thousand vibrations per second makes the highest audible sound. For some time scientists have been experimenting with sound, or rather soundless, waves that vibrate at a rate far above that of the highest audible waves. They have made some exceedingly interesting discoveries, such as the speed with which the higher frequencies can kill bacteria and otherwise affect matter.

"However, to get to the point, I have, by means of a special electromagnet, and a quartz tube of my own invention, succeeded in producing sound waves that vibrate at the inconceivable rate of eighty-seven thousand vibrations per second!"

Buddy regarded him with a bored air. "So what?" he inquired.

The professor controlled with difficulty an impulse to shake him, but continued calmly, "I have found that these waves exert a strange effect upon matter subjected, under certain conditions, to their influence."

For the first time his son evinced interest. "How can they do that?" he asked excitedly, his eyes shining. "And what—"

"Hold on a moment," said his father, smiling in spite of himself. "I'll explain. It seems that the sound waves affect in some way the nucleus of the atom. They increase its positive charge, and the free electrons which are held in their orbits because of the balance maintained between the pull of the vastly larger nucleus, and the centrifugal force that is a result of their motion, are drawn into new orbits which are closer to the nucleus, thus decreasing the size of the atom as a whole."

"Why don't the electrons crash into the nucleus and neutralize its positive charge with their negative charges?"

Professor Allen looked surprised. "So you do know *something*!" he exclaimed. "They don't fall into the nucleus because the speed they gain by falling to their new orbits increases their centrifugal force enough to enable them to withstand its attraction. Do you get it?"

"I believe so—"

"Then come here and look into this microscope."

Buddy walked over to where the professor was standing and peered into the large compound microscope. He saw what appeared to be a section of an exceedingly stagnant lake, in which were swimming numberless little creatures.

"Do you see those large slipper-shaped things that move with a spiral, rapid motion?" inquired his father.

"Yes. What are they, some kind of fish?"

Professor Allen snorted. "Fish nothing!" he snapped. "They're infinitely lower in the scale than fish. They belong to the group known to zoologists as Protozoa, and they consist of but a single cell."

"Gee! And they swim just like little fish—or bugs. What's that little one shaped sort of like a kidney?"

"That's also a Protozoan. Oxytricha is its name. And the almost colorless ones that change shape so often are amoebae. Now come over here and take a peek into this one," he gestured toward a second large instrument that stood upon a laboratory bench, "and prepare for a surprise, young fellow." His voice sounded triumphant.

Buddy immediately moved over to the bench and glanced obligingly into the microscope. After gazing into it for a moment he looked up inquiringly and said, "I don't see anything different here. There's only the same bunch of Paramecia and other things."

The professor pushed him aside and changed the position of the slide. "Take a good look at that piece of vegetation in the center of the field," he said, and his voice shook slightly.

Buddy again put his eye to the instrument. A second later he gave vent to a loud exclamation. "Good God!" he cried. "There's a yellow cat down there! Why, it looks like your cat Rubidium!"

"Quite so," agreed his father, with a quiet smile. "I reduced her to that size by means of the high frequency sound waves we were discussing a while ago."

"But how—I mean—can she get back?"

"I believe so. I was just going to find out when you broke in. You see, my experiments have shown me that whether the waves enlarge or reduce any object in their path depends upon the manner in which the waves are employed. If the waves are started at a low rate of vibration which is gradually increased, they will a have a reducing effect. However, if they are started at once at a high rate, which is then slowly decreased, they will enlarge matter. Now, if you don't mind, I'll continue with the experiment."

He picked up a pair of tweezers that had exceedingly fine tips, and gently lifted the minute cat, depositing the bewildered feline upon a small piece of paper. This he carried over to a complicated apparatus which Buddy had not before noticed. The invention consisted externally of a large electromagnet to which was fastened a queerly shaped tube, apparently of quartz. One end of the tube was fashioned into a large convex lens which helped to direct the waves into a concave reflector of metal. It was a few inches away from this reflector that the tip of the tweezers containing the struggling cat was held. Professor Allen then touched a button upon the wall near the machine. Instantly the great magnet began to vibrate, slowly at first, but with the rate constantly increasing.

"I am increasing the voltage slowly," explained the professor. An almost inaudible hum was coming from the contrivance, and before Buddy's startled eyes the tip of the tweezers began to enlarge rapidly. Within moments there lay between two great coarse points of metal a full-sized house cat, mewing its discomfort plaintively, until it fell to the floor, and scuttled under a bench.

Buddy stared at his father with something like awe in his gaze. "Could you do that to a man?" he demanded in an excited voice.

"I think so. Why?"

"Was that why you seemed so interested in my desire for adventure? Do you plan to—?"

"Yes."

"Would you—that is—could I come along?" Buddy blurted out.

Professor Allen's face became serious, almost grim. "There would be much scientific data of great value to acquire," he said, "but it would be a very dangerous thing to attempt."

"Who cares?" cried his son boyishly. "What an adventure! It would make tiger hunting look tame! "Death in a Drop," or "Pounced on by a Paramecium!"" Then he became serious. "Can we really go?" he asked. "And when do we start?"

"We *can* go," stated Professor Allen, "and we will—tomorrow."

On the following morning, all was in readiness for the start. Behind the doors of the laboratory, the final instructions were being given to Keeton, who was to handle things at that end.

The professor was speaking: "Now John, here's what you're to do. I have fixed the timer on the machine so that at the end of five minutes we shall have decreased to a height of about an inch. The switch will then turn off the current automatically. Incidentally, our inflatable rubber boat will be also reduced, along with these paddles. When we are one inch in height, place us carefully upon a glass slide and turn on the current. Allow it to remain on for five seconds—absolutely no longer! Then carry the slide gently over to the microscope and tilt it so that we may slide or crawl off alongside the specially prepared drop. At the end of two hours, look for us with a good magnifying glass; we'll be at the edge of the drop near the slide. We'll get on the slide, and you will then reverse the process, but don't forget to start the vibrations at a low rate and to slowly increase it. Got all that straight?"

"Yes, professor."

"I say, Dad," inquired Buddy, "how do you keep the waves from enlarging objects beyond the one on which they are focused?"

"The waves themselves are rather weak," explained his father. "They are concentrated by that metal reflector there, and nothing past the focal point of the reflector receives enough of the waves to be affected. Well, let's go." He took his place opposite the large reflector and as Buddy stepped to a position alongside, threw over the switch.

Buddy felt his body vibrate at a rate that seemed to shatter his bones. In a surprisingly short time it was over. For a few moments, the walls of the laboratory, with their well-filled shelves, seemed to leap upward and recede. Presently the impression of motion ceased. He then felt a sickening sensation at the pit of his stomach as he was whisked through the air and placed upon a large glass platform, which he knew to be the three-inch long slide. He could see plainly upon its surface, large bits of material that remained after a perfunctory wiping. With a smile he noted how uneven its surface appeared.

He grinned at his father, who was tightly clutching the light paddles, and as he did so, the upward leap of the walls recommenced. Almost instantly their apparent motion ceased; Buddy and his father were now less than one-fiftieth of an inch in height, respectively. Again Buddy felt himself, along with the slide, raised what seemed to be miles in the air. The walls of the laboratory were barely discernable in the distance as great dim barriers. "Ballooning has nothing on this!" he thought.

Abruptly the slide tilted at an acute angle, and they slid down to a position along the shore of a great lake. And what a densely populated lake it was! In every direction the eye could see queer creatures making the water boil with their rapid motion. Buddy pointed with a shaking finger to where a great elongated jelly-like monster was making the water foam with lashing strokes of its slightly flattened tentacles. From their new perspective, the creature appeared to be about eight feet long, and it swam with an odd spiral motion.

"What is it?" Buddy asked, his face white.

"That's what you were watching so smugly a while ago," retorted Professor Allen. "That's a Paramecium." The animal ceased its forward motion for a few moments, while a membrane-like group of fused tentacles, or cillia, propelled bits of organic material down its oral groove and into its gullet.

Suddenly Buddy and his father were aware of the presence of another of the denizens of the drop, somewhat smaller than the Paramecium, but with the suggestion about it of an intensely carnivorous animal. It was more rounded, and had at its anterior end a tube-like projection that reminded Buddy of the proboscis of a cotton boll weevil.

"Didinium!" cried the professor. "He's going to attack the Paramecium."

The ferocious creature circled about the larger animal for a moment as if to get its bearings, before closing viciously in.

When it was within several feet of its prey, the latter seemed to explode. From all parts of its body there shot out great masses of thick, sticky threads, which surrounded the Didinium and forced it back, hopelessly entangled. Then the victorious infusorian made off, spiraling through the water with unthinkable speed.

"Whew!" gasped the younger Allen. "What happened then?"

Professor Allen ran one hand through his shock of red hair, and gave Buddy a delighted grin. "The Paramecium was defending itself by means of those sticky threads, which are called trichocysts. They are contained in the cortex layer of its body, and expand when the Paramecium is excited or in danger. You see they're quite effective, and luckily too, for the Didinium is a great destroyer of Paramecia. In fact it's probably their worst enemy. This one got fooled though; he never knew what hit him. Well, let's launch our noble craft and be off; we've no time to waste if we're to make that island out there." The professor gestured with a paddle toward a large low-lying island, which—to their newly adjusted senses—appeared to be about three miles out.

Thus admonished, Buddy set up the light rubber boat and in a short time they had it inflated and launched, with Buddy wielding the paddles.

As they left the shore behind, the scene became more and more wonderful. The lake was alive with the lower forms of life, which swam in all sorts of odd ways in its odorous and cluttered waters. For the first time they noticed a peculiar visual effect due to the fact that the light was coming to their eyes after passing through the drop of water. There was no light at all reaching them from above.

Once Buddy lay down the paddles while they watched with great interest the manner in which a large Paramecium was dividing in two. First the two nuclei, the large and the small, divided, forming daughter nuclei. A new gullet budded off from the old one, and then a slight constriction of the whole body was followed by its division into two parts, each of which swam briskly off, later to repeat the process.

When they were within a few hundred yards of the island, the stench of which was sickening, Buddy caught sight of a strange animal that was walking slowly along the lake bottom. Through the murky water he could see that the grainy looking jelly-like creature was moving by means of large fleshy projections of its body. When he showed his find to his father, the latter identified it as an amoeba.

"It actually walks," explained the professor. "You see it extends a projection, a pseudopod as it is called, and attaches it to some point ahead. It then contracts the rest of its body and draws up to the point of attachment. That it does walk, instead of roll, is a recent discovery by a man named Dellinger."

As he spoke, the boat drew up to the island and with a light spring, Buddy landed upon the spongy vegetable soil. He then turned about and drew the vessel out of the water, at which point the professor stepped out.

Even as they landed, the island quivered under them in a strange fashion. A short glance about showed them the cause. On three sides of the island its shores were being attacked by hundreds of Protozoans, all of various types. The vegetable tissue was perfectly suited to their palates and they devoured it rapidly. Amoebae engulfed loose bits; paramecia brushed off rotting fragments, and on all sides the water swarmed with more inconspicuous species.

"Talk about the starving millions!" laughed Buddy. "These things look as though they haven't had a square meal for ages!"

"Their life consists only of eating and reproducing," stated his father.

Buddy suddenly uttered a cry. "Look there!" he shouted. "A monster snake!"

Professor Allen whirled about and saw a giant red-spotted snake that was covered with bristling, stiff hairs. As he watched, the great animal heaved its ponderous body on to the island, causing it to quiver perceptibly.

"That's some kind of annelid worm!" snapped Professor Allen in an alarmed tone. "Let's go back a few yards."

To their horror, the giant worm followed them in a seemingly aimless, but nevertheless menacing fashion. The professor whipped out the heavy automatic that hung at his waist, and fired twice, his last shot blending with that of Buddy's. The terrible creature whipped about in pain for a few moments, and then continued to advance, its lowly nervous system as yet functioning. A carefully placed shot by the elder Allen pierced its minute brain, and it writhed about in its death throes.

"These creatures have great powers of regeneration," said the professor, as he studied the dying worm from a safe distance. "They're like earthworms in that respect. Also, notice how translucent they are. You can see this one's intestine and the blood vessels parallel to it."

As the gigantic annelid was now dead, they moved closer for a more minute examination. The professor pointed to the stiff black "hairs" that grew in profusion all over the worm's body. "Those are called "setae,"" he said. "It is due to their number that this animal belongs to the subclass Polychaeta, meaning "many bristles.""

Buddy left the professor studying the worm's body while he went over to the water's edge. He stooped and regarded the liquid closely. Swimming in its dirty depths were countless little animals resembling tiny octopi. Buddy called to Professor Allen in a puzzled tone. "Hey, Dad, come here a minute will you? There's some kind of little animal here that looks like an octopus."

Professor Allen reluctantly left the carcass of the annelid worm and went over to where Buddy was gazing into the evil-smelling water. He peered into the filthy liquid and started.

"By heaven!" he gasped. "Typhoid Bacilli!"

"You mean those are germs?"

"Exactly. Those thin lengthy tentacles are the creatures' flagella; whip-like processes that propel them through the water."

As the professor studied the bacteria with professional interest, Buddy's attention was attracted by a rather small, spindle-shaped animal that was moving slowly through the water by means of a single long flagellum. He tapped his father upon the shoulder and pointed toward the odd creature. "Do you know what that one is?" he inquired.

The professor glanced at the animal and laughed.

"Know it?" he chuckled. "There isn't a zoologist or botanist in the world who doesn't. It's a Euglena, and no one knows whether it's a plant or an animal. You see, it moves like an animal, indeed it has an animal's mouth, and yet it manufactures its food like a plant. Its green color is caused by the chlorophyll contained in special bodies called "chromatophores." By means of its chlorophyll it manufactures starch just like a plant."

They watched the green, graceful creature as it cruised about in the water, occasionally taking food into its mouth. Suddenly Buddy whirled about, his face white.

"My God! Look there!" he roared.

The professor turned quickly, his hand on his revolver. As he caught sight of the thing, he gasped. It was a great jointed animal, covered with thick shiny armor that made it look like an animated tank. It had two great hairy antennae, by means of which it swam at a remarkable rate of speed. The posterior part of its huge body consisted mainly of two large transparent oval cases that were filled with rounded eggs.

"Heavens!" the professor cried. "Now we *are* in for it. That's a female Cyclops, a genus of Class Crustacea, and she's the biggest thing in this drop!"

The giant crustacean crashed its immense armored body against the island, causing the latter to tremble throughout. A large section of the rotting vegetation was torn loose and hurled yards away.

"We'd better beat it!" Professor Allen roared into Buddy's ear, for the crash of the waves created by the motion of the Cyclops drowned out anything said in a conversational tone.

As quickly as possible they launched the rubber boat, and with Buddy paddling furiously they set out upon the return journey. With a sinking feeling they saw the monster crustacean return and sweep around their frail craft, almost swamping it with the great waves caused by its rapid motion.

Buddy fired his automatic twice. To his amazement, the heavy bullets merely glanced off the Cyclops' thick covering.

"Aim for its eye," shouted his father, pointing towards the glowing red spot in the center of its anterior segment. Buddy did so, and the sparkling spot winked out. With a rush the giant, maddened animal whipped past their boat. The frail ship stood on end, seemed to hang poised in the air, and then returned with a jar to an even keel.

"One more like that and we're through!" yelled Buddy, wielding the paddles with all his strength. Again the blind monster, shooting by, missed the boat by inches. One great antenna knocked a paddle from Buddy's grasp and hurled it a hundred feet away.

With the single remaining paddle he again began to propel the violently lurching craft toward the nearby shore, where lay the glass slide. Then, to their horror and fear, the Cyclops hurled its enormous impregnable body directly at the boat. Even as it approached them with unthinkable speed, Buddy and his father heard a distant roar as if a giant hand was emptying a great bucket of some liquid into the waters of the lake. Immediately the gigantic, rushing Cyclops stiffened and ceased its forward motion, and its great armored carcass drifted up to the very gunwales of their boat. It was stone dead.

Buddy immediately resumed his one-oared paddling, and in a short while they landed upon the shore on which the large glass slide was lying. As they took their places upon its surface, they noticed that the large lake was strangely quiet; its waters were no longer being churned up by great numbers of animals. Here and there, a Paramecium would swim sluggishly a yard or two, only to lie still a second later.

Then came the hum of the generator, and no sound had ever been so sweet.

A short time later, they stepped from beneath the large polished reflector, and shook hands heartily with old Keeton. The latter was deathly pale, the result of their narrow escape, he explained.

"That Cyclops almost had you!" he blurted out.

"Was it you that finished the thing?" demanded Buddy, himself a trifle pale, and as Keeton nodded, asked, "How on earth did you do it?"

"I put a pipette-full of mercuric chloride into the other end of the drop," explained the old man, smiling.

Buddy looked about the laboratory and sighed.

"Boy!" he exclaimed. "Whoever said that scientists led quiet lives was sure barking up the wrong tree. They don't watch funny little animals under a microscope, heck no! They go down and kick the darn things around!"

# Monsters of the Grasslands

A rapidly swelling sound not unlike that of an airplane engine first recalled Dick McCrae to the horror of his predicament. His hasty upward glance disclosed a sight that frosted the very marrow of his bones. Hovering a scant few feet above his head, motionless save for the humming beat of gauzy, iridescent wings, a nightmarish monster surveyed him from two great, faceted eyes—eyes as soulless as those of the Devil himself.

With a choked cry Dick whirled and ran, scarcely realizing the uselessness of such a maneuver. A net-like plant entangled his flying feet, and he fell heavily to the ground. The flying monster swooped toward him, buzzing shrilly. Now it was just above the prostrate man, and McCrae saw the jointed abdomen double back, saw a yellow poison globule ooze from the end of a great, quivering sting. Just as he gathered his forces for a hopeless battle, there was a swish of mighty pinions, and the wasp was gone, struggling feebly in the beak of a dusty grey bird.

Hurriedly scrambling to his feet, McCrae resumed his frantic flight to the sanctuary of a cave he had glimpsed in the mighty cliff before him—a cliff that was actually a small bit of rock.

Once in the clear, the hunting wasp had brought home to him the terrors of his reduction. Now, in the cave, his scientific training insisted that he take stock, and consider what was to be done.

First, there was the matter of fire. Fire to cook his food and keep dangerous animals from his cave. A search of his pockets disclosed not a single match. Here was a pretty pass. Dressed in ordinary street clothes, no matches, and set down in the midst of the most savage jungle one could imagine—the insect grasslands! McCrae's examination did bring forth, however, his watch, which like practically all matter was affected by the ray. McCrae wished bitterly that the special boron glass used by Professor Gordon in the ray-tube had also reduced and spoiled the experiment. A careful scrutiny of the watch crystal disclosed that it was convex enough to serve as a sun-glass. That would do for fire.

Then there was the question of food, which also indicated a need for weapons. McCrae shuddered; he'd hate to face another wasp without a weapon.

Late in the afternoon, when many of the predatory insects were discouraged by the cooling earth, Dick left his cave and set about to acquire first a weapon, and then food.

A broken bit of stone served as a makeshift bludgeon, but food was not forthcoming. Several times McCrae stalked small grasshoppers, but to no avail; the wary insects soared high into the air on his approach.

At length McCrae found a berry bush at the foot of which lay several ripe berries. Eagerly he attacked the red, twenty-four inch spheres. Never had any fruit tasted so good.

As he was finishing his vegetarian dinner, an inquisitive head peered about a nearby grass blade to be followed soon by an immense, armored body. McCrae recognized the clumsy creature at once. It was a pill bug; not an insect, but a crustacean that had forsaken its watery habitat eons before. Dick knew it to be comparatively harmless, feeding largely on humus, but the sight of its mighty cuirass stirred his fertile imagination.

Clutching his stone club, he stalked the dull-witted giant and delivered a crushing blow upon its small head. The great crustacean reared in pain, probing blindly for its assailant. McCrae delivered blow after blow, dancing out of reach each time, and in a few moments the animal lay motionless.

Although it was getting dark, Dick knew that he must remove the pill bug's armor at once; the ravenous red ants would make short work of the carcass were it left there.

Fortunately McCrae was able to find a sharp-edged bit of glassy silica. With its aid, he soon removed several of the light, tough chitinous plates. These he carried to his cave, together with a bundle of sticks and some stringy grass blades.

As it was too late to do anything about a fire, Dick piled boulders in the entrance, threw himself upon the hard floor, and slept like one dead.

Early the next morning found him hard at work upon the sticks. It took much laborious scraping and experimentation, but at length McCrae succeeded in turning out a passable looking bow-stave, almost as good as the lemon-wood one with which he'd won the archery tournament some years before. From the grass blades he extracted enough fibers to make a tough, flexible bowstring; while other sticks served for sharp, featherless arrows.

As he gathered up his equipment and moved toward the mouth of the cave to test his sun-glass, the boulders were swept aside like so much chaff, and a terrifying figure darkened the entrance.

McCrae's widened eyes took in the great, globular body, the eight hairy legs, the compound and simple eyes, and above all the clashing, poisoned mandibles, and his heart sank. A hunting spider was preparing to invade his cave!

Backing slowly away, McCrae fitted an arrow to his bow. The tough wood bent almost double as he drew the arrow far back. As the monster crouched for the irresistible spring of the predatory spider, the heavy pointed stick streaked through the air to bury itself in a crystalline eye.

It was a lucky shot that must have pierced the tiny brain, for the spider rolled over clawing frantically at the air. Lymph oozed from the punctured eye, and still in its death struggles the invader rolled away from the cave.

A week went by, during which time McCrae sought desperately for some way out of his awful predicament. No use to go near a man even if one should come to this isolated place. Towering hundreds of feet above the tiny McCrae, no man would even notice him. Indeed, he'd be more likely to crush him underfoot. McCrae could not even locate the house he had fled from; his reduction in size had cut down the range of his vision, and he was sadly muddled as to his position. He had mused often upon the paradox of his weight. Unless matter had been destroyed, he should weigh as much as he did when full size. But obviously he didn't; if he weighed that much his strength would have to be equal to supporting such a weight, and he had no evidence of such strength.

A month after the catastrophe that had befallen him, McCrae was ranging the grasslands more boldly, clad in armor belonging of late to a certain pill bug. He hoped that in the event of an attack by a stinging insect, it would ward off the sharp point until he could bring his weapons into play.

But those weapons had proven themselves very tricky. McCrae soon realized that only an eye shot could kill the average insect; the casing of tough chitin that guarded the rest of their bodies was too much for any pointed stick to pierce.

It had really been amusing, that first attempt. Tiring of his vegetarian diet, McCrae had decided to conquer his natural repugnance and try the flesh of an insect. There was only one common insect which might prove reasonably easy prey—the tiny green grasshopper of the grasslands. But tiny as it might be, it was fully as large as a cow to Dick, and was armored as no cow had ever been. McCrae had stalked the nervous insect for what seemed hours. Each time he got within range the grasshopper somehow spotted him, and its resulting leap seemed to carry it to the stratosphere. Then McCrae would make his laborious way through several hundred more feet of tangled underbrush, only to have the neurotic creature repeat its amazing leap.

But the worst part was that it had done him no good to get a shot at the confounded animal. When he had finally managed to creep close, he had fitted the sharpest, most carefully balanced arrow to the bow and sent it whizzing through the air. To his dismay, even though he had aimed for the comparatively soft abdomen, the arrow had glanced from the chitinous plates and soared off, while the startled grasshopper had doubled his previous leaps.

Pointed bits of stone, bound to arrows which boasted fibrous feathering, helped very little. What hope was there for a hunter, when some 'hopper with three arrows through various portions of its anatomy bounced about as full of life as ever, chewing leaves with perfect equanimity!

Once having succeeded in killing a particularly debilitated grasshopper, McCrae found, to his great delight, that a giant hind leg, roasted slowly over a fire, was fully as toothsome as the finest cut of lamb.

But it was on a later hunting expedition that he made his most important discovery. He'd been hiding from a praying mantis behind a crumbly ledge of some mineral deposit, waiting nervously for the weird monster with its cruel, saw-toothed arms to depart. Then the mineral had captured his attention, and the gasp he emitted almost betrayed him to the ravenous horror poised nearby.

McCrae was a zoologist, but in his search for rare animals he had had occasion to become familiar with many minerals, and this, by all the tea in China was saltpeter!

When the mantis stalked off upon the trail of a foolish caterpillar, McCrae filled his ever-present specimen sack with the precious stuff and hurried home. There in the back of his cave was a heap of crude sulfur, which McCrae had obtained with great labor from a nearby deposit of the native mineral. It took a drastic reduction in size to cultivate one's powers of observation; McCrae would have sworn the nearest saltpeter was in Kentucky—the nearest sulfur straight down!

Here then, were the means for the manufacture of the one weapon that could laugh at chitinous armor—a firearm. It took McCrae many weary hours to find a wood that could be made into moderately good charcoal, but at length the three heaps stood side by side in the cave— saltpeter, sulfur, and charcoal. McCrae could have cried for joy ...

But the preparation of the mixture; how easy it looked in textbooks, and how difficult it was in practice. Time after time the product came out lumpy and slow burning. Experience, however, led to improvement; the moistened ingredients, ground together to microscopic fineness and carefully dried, flared encouragingly beneath the sun-glass.

The manufacture of a firearm proved even more difficult; there was not a scrap of metal to be had. McCrae bethought him of the leather canon in use centuries earlier, but the toughest leaves he could find—leaves in appearance like great sheets of green leather—split like tissue paper under the pressure of the super-heated gases of combustion.

McCrae was not to be daunted, however. He hollowed out a bit of wood, using a heated splinter of stone to char the unwanted center away. Using threads from his clothes, and sacrificing his single remaining shoelace, he bound and rebound the barrel of his crude wooden pistol to withstand the powder charge. The result was a crude caricature of a pirate's handgun in appearance. In performance, with a heavy charge of homemade powder, and a pebble in the muzzle, the weapon delighted McCrae. So much so, in fact, that he constructed a rifle upon the same plan—a rifle that shot with moderate accuracy for a distance of fifty feet, and with sufficient power to pierce a half-inch of wood.

The first grasshopper hunt was a joy. A powder horn of leaf at his belt, a pocket full of round pebbles, and his guns loaded and patched, McCrae, with a finesse born of practice, stalked a great, foolishly chewing grasshopper.

When he attained a position some fifteen feet away, McCrae sighted along the slightly wavy barrel and fired; that is to say, he held a bit of burning punk to a tiny hole in the breech. To his great glee the clearing smoke revealed the grasshopper lying helplessly upon the ground, a great gash in its thoracic armor. The shocking power of the heavy pebble made even a comparatively slight wound effective.

McCrae surveyed his prize proudly, unaware that he too was being stalked. A slight rustling first shook him from his reverie. He whirled about, drawing the pistol as he did so, and faced his stalker. The sight that met his eyes was enough to congeal his blood. Fully twenty feet long it stood, its vast bulk supported by dozens of agile legs. Below its blank, faceted eyes, two great, razor-edged mandibles clashed together menacingly. McCrae well knew that no mere pistol shot would stop this monster; it was a centipede; an animal possessed of unbelievable vitality and the will of an Epictetus.

But there was nothing else to do; running would be an utterly useless maneuver. The centipede is a greyhound among the arthropods. The pistol boomed, and a weighty pebble tore into the first segment, ripping away a leg. The colossus seemed unaware of its wound, and gathered itself for the charge.

At that moment there was an unexpected interruption. A great buzzing shape landed squarely upon McCrae, crushing him heavily to the ground. The sickening stench of carrion filled his nostrils; he was veritably enclosed by a fence of six hairy, filth-clotted legs.

A giant bluebottle fly had landed directly upon him. But not for long. Catching sight of the momentarily confused centipede, a horrible enemy of his race, the bluebottle emitted a shrill buzz of terror and leaped into the air. He did not go alone; in an agony of fear, McCrae seized a thick, jointed leg and held on. Despite the bluebottle's frantic efforts to rid itself of the clinging mite, the man clutched desperately to the leg. As it retracted for ease in flight, McCrae found a perch in the crook of the bent limb.

For what seemed centuries McCrae remained in his perilous position, while the stupid fly buzzed aimlessly around in acute dismay. As they hurtled breathtakingly about McCrae's fevered brain wondered. If he were to lose his hold would he fall lightly, without harm, as all insects do, or would he drop as a man does from an airplane, with sickening acceleration to death? Logically he was as light as any insect, and air resistance should break his fall, but McCrae had no inclination to put the matter to a test.

Suddenly the bluebottle dropped with nauseating velocity toward a great flat plane below. Cautiously it buzzed about the smooth surface; McCrae was in an agony of suspense. Then with a last buzz, the fly made a six-point landing squarely upon the surface. For a second it stood motionless, then its powerful wings beat the air in a mad flurry. But to no avail; the bluebottle was held firmly by a swampy plane that stretched for endless yards. McCrae fell from his perch into the semi-liquid mess and laughed hysterically. They were trapped on a sheet of flypaper. Abruptly a black pall swept over him.

Dick McCrae opened his eyes to look directly into those of Professor Gordon. "What—" Dick began.

"Don't try to talk," the professor cautioned him. "Take it easy; looks like you've had quite a time. You know, I almost took you for a bug with that armor you had on."

"I've got to talk!" cried McCrae. "How did I get back?"

"That fly carried you in here."

"But you; I thought you—"

"No. After the flames reached me, I must have revived in a hurry. I grabbed the extinguisher and checked the fire. I looked everywhere for you, but it was no use; you were so small. I thought you'd burned in the fire. I tell you, Dick, I suffered."

"*You* suffered! Why for—"

"I know; you blame me. But when that insect brought you here, I felt like turning it loose in the sugar bowl."

"You wouldn't say that if you knew how it smelled."

Gordon did not smile. "I hope you can forgive me, Dick," he said pleadingly. "I'll even destroy the ray-tube if you want me to."

"Like hell you will. That's scientific sabotage! But I will forgive you—on one condition."

"Yes, Dick?"

"That you let me go back with a few hand-grenades and a machine gun. I want to show those damned bugs who's boss." He paused, smiling. "Just kidding. But say, before I tell you my story, how is it you said my weight would remain the same? It didn't!"

The professor flushed. "It's—er—a matter of higher mathematics, Dick. As a zoologist you couldn't follow—"

Dick chuckled. "We'll skip that. But let me tell you this: next time you have at least eight heart specialists and four assistants here, or it's no go!"

# The Soulless Ones: Vespa

It was cruelly hot in the dusty field. The vertical rays of a July sun beat down with an intensity that was almost physical pressure. Yet life was astir in the baking grassroots: life, industrious in many strange ways, talented at birth, and completely ruthless, knowing only the inflexible law of instinct pattern ...

Moving purposefully through the weedy growth was a fantastic figure, slender and sinister, with a pointed, inquisitive head set on a body carried nearly upright by its rearmost two pairs of legs. Its folded forelegs were poised aloft in an attitude suggestive of pious supplication, a position which gave no hint of their murderous potentialities, and its gossamer, green wings, like the finest silk, trailed at its sides. Of all insects, this one alone has the power to turn its head and direct its basilisk gaze.

Abruptly the creature paused and stiffened, as its searching glance fell upon a small, green grasshopper, drunk with the sun-ecstasy, which, except for mating, is the insect's sole joy in life. The gauzy wings of the slender huntress unfurled themselves to shoot up in a spectrally menacing gesture until they were almost parallel above her head. Simultaneously, the tip of her snaky abdomen curled over her back to scrape raspingly against the rough nervures of an extended wing. Thus does the praying mantis add terror to her relentless attack.

If the sun-intoxicated grasshopper experienced any fear at the impressive sight, there was no sign of it in the blank, foolish eyes. Only when the long forelegs of the mantis extended themselves with startling rapidity to reveal a double row of spines on the inner surfaces of each joint, did the frightened victim tense its practiced jumping-legs. Too late! Gripped by the needle-pointed grappling hook at the end of each foreleg, and drawn into the deadly spiked V's of the joints, to be pierced through and through its soft body, the grasshopper was quickly dispatched by a deliberate munching of its neck, a coolly-performed act which destroyed the vital nerve center there.

Unhampered now by any frantic struggling, the mantis calmly devoured the corpse; little driblets of flesh occasionally fell from her mumbling jaws. Everything was eaten except the dry wings, which were flung carelessly aside to be scorned even by the eager red ants.

It was then that Vespa, the hunting wasp, took a hand in the grim game. She had been rocking on powerful wings, happy in the fierce caress of the sun, yet anxious for the eggs in her teeming womb, when her soulless, faceted eyes spied the little drama being enacted in the grass below. She was a born mantis hunter, and that dangerous insect held little terror for the clockwork of her minute brain. Like a tiny Stuka, she hurtled downward, and although she rarely made a sound in flight, she buzzed with shrill, menacing intensity as she zoomed past the startled mantis.

But the threat of her vibrant war cry daunted the ferocious insect only momentarily. Her wicked little head pivoted in an almost human movement, as she peered up to locate the aerial attacker, and she reared to do desperate battle with the murderous, spiny traps of her shears opening and closing with fierce eagerness.

Again Vespa buzzed down, only to swerve off before the soundless warning of the mantis' terrible weapons; and, as if to prepare for the inevitable struggle, the keen point of her dagger unsheathed itself to display a glistening droplet of venom on its tip.

Had Vespa wished merely to kill the praying mantis, her task would have been comparatively simple. A single lightning thrust of the envenomed dagger into any vital spot, and the mantis, for all her bulk, would have twitched out her life in a very few seconds. But the wasp's purpose in engaging her foe was much more subtle—and horrible. It was essential that her prey should not die instantly; it should merely be so paralyzed that Vespa's larva might feed on fresh food—living food, in fact—but food incapable of any writhings dangerous to the life of the feeble infant.

Without warning, Vespa ceased her jockeying for position to drop with baffling rapidity high on the mantis' body. Her mandibles gripped the neck; her six legs twined hastily about the struggling creature, and her abdomen, bearing the ready sting, curled forward and under to plunge the dagger deep into the nerve center controlling the mantis' formidable weapons. Instantly the spiked forelegs, already seeking the wasp's frail body, dropped lifelessly to the insect's sides. Quickly but methodically, Vespa slid down her victim's back as a man slides down a pole, her stiletto again ready. As she reached a position directly above the middle pair of legs, her sting plunged in once more, and moving still lower, she delivered a final, vicious thrust to the ganglion of the last two legs.

With the completion of the last of Vespa's trio of devastating thrusts, the mantis collapsed limply into an inert hulk, capable only of a disorganized twitching which rapidly decreased in violence and extent.

Nonchalantly, as if defeating a monster many times her own bulk and armed to the teeth were an everyday occurrence—which indeed it was—Vespa seized the paralyzed mantis with her six legs and vigorously took flight, the long limbs of her prize trailing loosely beneath her.

At a spot on the ground indistinguishable, to human eyes, at least, from any other, Vespa alighted with her clumsy burden, depositing it carefully to one side while she scraped away enough loose earth to disclose the mouth of a tunnel dug some hours earlier. Into this she backed, laboriously dragging the inert insect after her. Once in the chamber at the end of the shaft, with scarcely a ray of light to guide her, Vespa laid a single egg, which she glued to her victim at a point destined to demonstrate her consummate knowledge of mantis anatomy. A few moments later, she emerged and set about concealing the entrance to the gallery containing her precious egg. This she quickly accomplished by using her nimble legs to cover the small opening with loose, dry earth. With an inspiration rare in insects, she seized a tiny pebble in her jaws and hammered down the soil in and about the mouth of the tunnel.

Then, with a single triumphant buzz, she launched herself into the sunshine she loved ...

And down in the blackness of the well-sealed shaft, the single egg, fastened with miraculous insight to the paralyzed mantis, soon hatched. A tiny, worm-like grub, all mouth and intestine, emerged to pierce the helpless monster's body and feed on its still-living flesh. With nature-bestowed skill, the grub devoured the mantis' non-essentials first—the fatty tissues, and the organ integuments—a process made possible only by the mother's judicious lodging of the egg. Gradually the mantis became an empty mockery, kept alive only through the grub's instinctive avoidance of the victim's few really vital organs.

Fresh meat to the very last, that is Vespa's creed, and not until the prolonged meal was almost complete, did the sated grub attack the vitals of the living mantis. A dead insect is a useless insect to the wasp larva, for it cannot feed on corruption.

The following spring, there issued from the hidden tunnel, after a long sleep by the empty husk of a large mantis, a newly-transformed wasp, which soon launched itself eagerly into the warm sunshine ...

What happened then, is, in the words of a great storyteller, a different story—albeit a very similar one.

# About the Author

Arthur Porges was born in Chicago, Illinois on August 20, 1915. One of four brothers, he was educated at The Illinois Institute of Technology where he achieved a Masters Degree in Mathematics. During the Second World War he served in the U.S. Army as an instructor, stationed for some time at the Camp White military installation in Oregon and at Barnes Hospital in Vancouver, Washington. After the war Porges moved to California and spent several years in Los Angeles as a mathematics teacher at college level. During this period he wrote and sold short stories as a sideline. In 1957, Porges retired from teaching to write full-time. He went on to publish hundreds of short stories in numerous magazines and newspapers. Many of his stories appeared in *Alfred Hitchcock's Mystery Magazine*, *Ellery Queen's Mystery Magazine*, *Amazing Stories* and *The Magazine of Fantasy and Science Fiction*. His fiction spanned several genres, with tales ranging from science fiction and fantasy to horror, mysteries, and so on. At his most prolific his work was appearing in three or four periodicals in one month alone. Among his best known stories are "The Ruum," "The Rats," "No Killer Has Wings," "The Mirror" and "The Rescuer." Four previous book collections of his short stories have been published: *Three Porges Parodies and a Pastiche* (1988), *The Mirror and Other Strange Reflections* (2002), *Eight Problems in Space: The Ensign De Ruyter Stories* (2008) and *The Adventures of Stately Homes and Sherman Horn* (2008). A keen birdwatcher and an avid reader, Porges also wrote many articles, essays and poems, most of which were published in *The Monterey Herald*. After spells in Laguna Beach and San Clemente, Porges moved north, eventually settling in Pacific Grove. He passed away, at the age of 90, in May 2006.